cat flap

cat flap

alan s. cowell

st. martin's press ✻ new york

CAT FLAP. Copyright © 2018 by Alan Cowell. All rights reserved. Printed in the United States of America. For information, address St. Martin's Press, 175 Fifth Avenue, New York, N.Y. 10010.

www.stmartins.com

Designed by Anna Gorovoy

Library of Congress Cataloging-in-Publication Data

Names: Cowell, Alan, author.
Title: Cat flap / Alan Cowell.
Description: First edition. | New York : St. Martin's Press, 2018.
Identifiers: LCCN 2017059651 | ISBN 978-1-250-14651-9
(hardcover) | ISBN 978-1-250-14652-6 (ebook)
Classification: LCC PR6103.O97 C37 2018 | DDC 823/.92—dc23
LC record available at https://lccn.loc.gov/2017059651

ISBN 978-1-250-20249-9 (international edition)

Our books may be purchased in bulk for promotional, educational, or business use. Please contact your local bookseller or the Macmillan Corporate and Premium Sales Department at 1-800-221-7945, extension 5442, or by email at MacmillanSpecialMarkets@macmillan.com.

First Edition: July 2018

10 9 8 7 6 5 4 3 2 1

For Cohli, Fizzfizz, Pina, and Nushi

cat flap

one

When she awoke as a cat, Dolores Tremayne saw no immediate advantage in having four paws instead of two arms and two legs; in being 100 percent swathed in fine, silky fur; in occupying the horizontal rather than the vertical plane; in having a tiny little sliver of pink tongue that attended willy-nilly to matters of intimate personal grooming. She did not know when the transformation, the metamorphosis, had occurred, or whether part of her was still human somewhere else in some other entity. She was aware of being incredibly small. She did not think right away of that book which opens with a man discovering that he has become a large and cumbersome insect lying on his hard, shell-like back in some indistinct faraway place. When she did think of him, she could not immediately recall his name. But she understood that she and he were different.

The man in the book was immobile. She was not. He was a monstrous bug. She was a cat. She moved, glided, rolled, scratched. She was aware of soft pads on rough sisal carpets, sharp claws digging into scratching posts in a place that she recognized as her own human home. She received signals, baffling at first, from her new whiskers, her nostrils, her enormous bushy tail.

A tail, for heaven's sake.

Samsa.

That was it. Gregor Samsa. She had not greatly enjoyed the book, despite the renown of its author, but her ability to remember it unsettled her.

If, as all evidence suggested, she was now a cat, how could she even begin to contemplate Mr. Samsa's predicament, for a cat's knowledge of nineteenth-century Czech authors—or any other authors or centuries for that matter—was, ipso facto, nonexistent. (If you don't agree, ask yourself when you last saw a cat leafing through *War and Peace,* or Gibbon's *The History of the Decline and Fall of the Roman Empire,* or even *Hello!* magazine.)

But if she had the kind of mind that could frame such conundrums, recall such factoids as the name of poor Gregor Samsa with relative—indeed, human—ease, why did she have the body of a cat?

Would a cat, even of the most superior and refined breeding, seek parallels in the words and works of Franz Kafka? (Once, on a business trip to Berlin, she had seen a plump tabby perched in the large plate-glass window of an artsy café, surrounded by colored posters for galleries and exhibits, as if claiming intimacy with Klimt and Macke. But that particular memory was from her human data banks—so how had they gotten into this cat's body?)

Would it help anyhow to compare her condition to that of some fictional character in a book that people only mentioned to show how smart they were, how well-read, well-bred? The analogy could only really help by suggesting that you were not alone, that your trans-species migration was not unique, that you were at the beginning of this, not the end. (Who remembers how *The Metamorphosis* ends? Not nicely is the answer.)

The reality was that, if you—or part of you—awoke as a cat; if the familiar orbit of your memory developed a sudden dark glitch, a hiccup, veering across uncharted reaches; if your entire life switched onto a different existential track as surely as an express train crossing the points at a critical junction between A and B hurtled off to destination C; if the entire trajectory of your achievements and status and pretensions and ambition became oddly irrelevant; then, if all or any of those conditions were your new self, you were entitled to all the help and solace you could get—from Franz Kafka, or Gregor Samsa, or anyone else you could summon to your banner.

Was it all a dream, derived from those questions of human, rather than feline, identity that seemed to trouble so many people? She thought she should pinch herself to see if she awoke. But tiny claws don't pinch. Only fingers pinch. And only humans and related primates had developed the exquisite motor skills of the opposable thumb, although many species have dreams that leave them twitching in their slumbers, legs and tails quivering in hidden pursuits and escapes. Only humans, as far as she knew, regarded self-pinching as a wake-up call. And if it was not a dream, there was nothing to wake up from.

Dolores Tremayne had walked out of her family apartment as a successful corporate executive, mou-mouing a kiss to her dashing husband, hugging their daughters, toting her laptop and carry-on, checking that she had credit cards, e-ticket printouts, frequent flier cards to permit access to comfortable lounges, her mind already reconnoitering the distant offices in Munich where she would negotiate a new contract for the supply of onboard computers and other electronic wizardry to enhance the experience of driving a top-of-the-line, fully-loaded, state-of-the-art BMW.

She had been wearing a tailored gray suit with not-too-high heels, a modest skirt and sheer stockings meant to emphasize her sculpted calves without seeming inappropriately flirtatious. Her deep-blue silk blouse was chosen to send the same message of attractiveness without immediate availability. (The bra and pants underneath from La Senza in Milan were her own affair.) Her agenda had been a construct of appointments, hotel accommodations, and flight reservations. (Business class, junior suite, she had told her secretary. Nothing too flashy for the eagle-eyed *tricoteuses* of Accounts.)

And, as far as her cat's eyes could intuit from her human absence in her human family home, Dolores Tremayne was still out there, over there, stepping off the Lufthansa flight, taking a Mercedes cab to the Hotel Vier Jahreszeiten, welcomed back by obsequious-arrogant concierges and front desk people, expressing herself fluently in German exchanges with a sly lilt of Bavarian— *Guten Tag! Wie geht's heute? Herzlich willkommen, gnaedige Frau! Schoen Sie wiederzusehen! Ebenfalls!*

But part of her was not there. Part of her—mind, soul, did the precise definition even matter?—had simply transferred, migrated or duplicated itself into the body of the finely bred, highly pedigreed family cat.

Part of her was X.

(Let's call her X, her youngest daughter, Astra, had said: she's a mystery cat. And the name had stuck, sounding somewhat precocious, it is true, but nonetheless appropriate in that North London environment where they take delight in such whimsy. Like teaching toddlers how to pronounce the word *diplodocus* with just the right modulation, or to spell *materialism* without necessarily knowing what it was.)

Apart from *The Metamorphosis,* she was also trying to recall the name of the movie about cats that includes a song with the line, sung by a cat: Everybody wants to be a cat.

Perhaps, she mused—or maybe mewed, or purred—everybody does want to be endowed with feline qualities of guile and superciliousness, of being able to manipulate the immediate environment to advantage. But when that wish is redeemed to its ultimate conclusion, the consequences are far more complicated than you might imagine.

When you are a cat, of course, you don't remember the titles of films because you cannot read the credits, you cannot really perceive things in the way humans do, have little sense of color (smell, night vision and hearing are different matters, oh yes!) and desire is limited to various reflexive moments rather than anticipating a pick-and-mix medley of pursuits that, based on previous experience or delicious anticipation, you would rather be engaged on, such as vacationing in Saint-Tropez or the Hamptons, or having sex, or imagining it while having dinner and

sipping fine Italian wine, as her human counterpart sometimes illicitly did on her business trips when a contact or
negotiator or counter-party requested an after-hours
pursuit of negotiations, discussions, "meetings," and, for
want of other amusement beyond room service and pay-
TV movies, she agreed to the first if never the second
sinful part of the evening's agenda.

Being a cat, in other words, should be enough in itself.
That is the central tenet of the feline universe. Unlike
lolloping, barking, bottom-sniffing, cock-tailing, tree-
peeing dogs, which seek codependency with their patrons,
cats are self-sufficient. They train their owners as their
personal attendants. They balance moments of affection
and phases of withdrawal. They share their logic with no
biped.

But life as a cat, Dolores was discovering, is not all saucers of milk and mindless games with feathery objects,
or chasing electronically-generated laser fish, or being
cuddly and loved unconditionally.

There is, for instance, the very simple question of
height. You live, almost literally, at ground level. Your
husband, wife, children rear above you, giants. You skulk
along skirting boards. Your neck arches ever upward,
craning in supplication to your benefactors. You are Lil-
liputian. Humiliated.

If, like X, you are a flat-cat, as locked into the family
apartment as surely as an orange-suited prisoner is con-
fined at Guantanamo Bay or Belmarsh high-security
prison in southeast London, a cat bred and destined to be
forever indoors, then your horizons extend no farther than
a carpet, and a scratch-post, and a ludicrous cat-tree that

resembles no natural tree in any way beyond vertical reach. For Hamptons, read: trip to the vet. Deworming, nail clipping, injections, fear and loathing of the white-jacketed torturer and extractor of enormous, unjustified fees. For sex, read nothing, not since one particular trip to the vet's after awakening to impossible, squirming, procreative urges, and the subsequent weight gain and loss of something that should never have been taken away— and certainly was not taken away from her human self, or from most of her more feral co-felines in gardens, along high walls, in shrubberies and nooks and crannies where natural instincts were allowed full, fecund yowling dominion.

Then there is communication. There they all are, thinking their spouse or parent is in Bavaria talking to German executives about GPS systems and USB ports and mp3 docks and Wi-Fi and The Cloud, and what can you say to disabuse them? I am here! Under your nose! Under your feet! Please do not tread on me! Look at me: only my physical appearance has changed! It is me! In the body of the cat you all love, or pretend to love.

Dolores Tremayne, it is true, could not resist a stirring of curiosity, befitting a cat, about the potential and limits of her new condition.

As a human, she had always kept herself in pretty good shape—gym subscriptions, jogging, the Dukan Diet had all seen to the business of maintaining a flattish stomach, an unembarrassing waist size for her purchases of houndstooth work suits and pricy logo-laden blue jeans, summer bikinis, winter ski suits, Indian Ocean wet suits. But she had never, before her life as a cat, experienced the tremendous, Ferrari-esque acceleration of four-legged power; the ability to leap into the air to heights double or triple the length of her own body (try jumping fifteen or eighteen feet in the air from a standing start, humans, even with a pole to help!); the ease with which, on silent paws, she could simply materialize at a junction of walls where she had not been a second earlier; or display the incredible lightness of her new being—and where did that phrase or something very like it come from?—springing over great canyons of sofas, descending, almost in glide-flight, from the polished surface of tables where she was not supposed to be in the first place. In short, she had never understood quadruped maneuverability, grace, until it was hers to inhabit.

(Now she was thinking of Orwell and *Animal Farm*—"four legs good, two legs bad!" How would a cat know that?)

But if her new maneuverability was the upside, the downside imposed itself in so many ways, such as eating when you have no hands, only paws that are no match for, say, a computer keyboard, or a knife and fork, or a pepper pot. Try poking your nose into a bowl of noisome pellets—the sole, no-star diet of a flat-cat—only at those preordained moments when food is made available by some higher being that used to be a husband or child.

Her vision, too, was fuzzy, warped, yet capable of functioning well in the dark (so it was true!) like those camera shots her human eyes used to follow in documentary television programs about benighted war zones or nocturnal watering holes in remote African game reserves when her huge, new, distant cousins slunk from the savannah to drink.

Her tiny, furry ears detected sounds much farther away than she had ever been able to hear. Her nostrils guided her with the same authority as the newest voice-activated, touch-screen gizmo fitted snugly into the dash of the 7 Series BMW in Munich.

And, as she was to discover, there was the supreme indignity of the toilet arrangements, entering a dark box, defecating in this artificial gloaming, scratching and shoveling to hide your embarrassment at the fact that there is no flush, no water, no paper—only the reliance on claw and paw.

Everybody wants to be a cat until they become one. *The Aristocats.*

That was the movie.

She prowled, now, below the lowest shelf of her bookcase. What would it be today? A dip into Kierkegaard? A sojourn with Wainwright in the Lake District? A little Dickens or Proust? Baudelaire? De Nerval? Lawrence? Dylan Thomas? T. S. fucking Eliot on the upper shelves located at eye level where her husband thought they advertised his wordy credentials?

Nothing, of course. Cats do not read. They cannot turn pages. (Cats do not swear, she reminded herself guiltily, anxious not to offend the norms of her breed, her fellow felines.)

Words blur, jumble—hieroglyphics, gradations of shade. Paper in its cardboard form is only of use for scratching and tearing when your nails need trimming—

another function she could no longer perform independently.

Sharing the body of X was like being in one of those dual-control cars used by driving schools, where the pupil may be happily barreling along with one wheel on a sidewalk and heading in the general direction of the rear of a bus when the instructor panics, grasps the wheel, slams on the brakes, cuts the engine, lights yet one more cigarette with shaking hands. (How could she have known that?)

X maintained her own volition, her own voice, her capricious sense of the appropriate moment for arrival or departure, sleep or wakefulness. X, more or less, was in the driver's seat. Dolores, more or less, was the passenger. X the instructor. Dolores the pupil. A cat in training, apprenticeship.

She found herself cleaning herself with her own tongue—Yeeuuww! She found herself contorting herself like a prepubescent Olympic gymnast, one leg extended vertically. She curled on beds. She lurked in dark corners.

As her elder daughter, Portia, switched on her laptop at a time Dolores gauged to be midway between several rather woozy naps (was this what was meant by catatonic?), she rested her head on the keyboard and peered at the screen but was aware of little more than the cursor, still less the incoming Facebook message asking her child for a clandestine meeting. ("I am 14-year-old girl just like you, will meet outside Kentish Town tube on Northern Line. Do not tell your parents.")

Get used to it, she tried to tell herself! You are a cat! Shit in a box! Slip through the cat flap in quest of company, new smells, mice, voles, pigeons, sparrows, rats—the whole menagerie of fluffy, furry, feathered beings that, according to human research, cats across the globe destroyed by the billion every year.

"But keep the dog far hence that's friend to man." At all costs. "Or with nails." Eliot. The top shelf that she could no longer reach.

Then she remembered that there was no cat flap. Dolores herself had taped the apartment's preexisting cat flap closed because X was a flat-cat, not a cat flap–cat like the downstairs neighbor's mischlings that set their own schedules and skulked and pooped around the communal gardens and returned from obscure nocturnal missions with limp, half-dead creatures in their jaws; or hurtled over the fence from Hampstead Heath with Labradors and Rottweilers in snarling, frustrated pursuit.

How long will I be a cat, Dolores found her human mind thinking as her feline body chose that very moment to approach an expensive sofa that she had selected in person from the top of the range at the Conran Shop in Marylebone High Street.

Systematically, dispassionately, X began to scratch the creamy fabric that she was not supposed to scratch.

Stop that, X, Dolores shouted silently, but her words had no effect.

How could they? She had no voice. The larynx belonged to X. Her feline side was unaware of her human side.

Dolores Tremayne had lost the biped right to dominance.

What will happen when my human body returns,

Dolores asked herself, when I come home from all the points on my extended business trip—Munich and Detroit and Tokyo? Do I nuzzle my own human legs with my furry cat flanks? And why oh why did I let them talk me into such an ambitious itinerary of long-haul flights and flat-bed seats and bratwurst and sushi and steaks the size of doormats? How can I tell me to come home?

Someone picked her up, tumbled her onto her back, rubbed her cozy, furry abdomen. She heard the sound of purring and realized that she was making it.

two

Although I was advertised as an indoor cat, one of a pedigreed litter from a breeder in Billericay, Essex—dewormed, house-trained, fully documented—part of me has defied this genetic tweaking and remains in thrall to the great outdoors, yearning for a breath of that free air, the comingling of diesel fumes and fox and dog and shoe and shit and mud that defines the world beyond the flat in which I am captive.

I suppose you would say this urge is a residual part of the DNA that links me to lions and tigers and the other truly big cats (big in the sense of absolute size rather than relatively big from regular free feeds in comparison with feral, street-smart versions of my species. Or big in the sense of plumpness requiring regular weigh-ins at the torture chamber of the white-coated bipeds who prescribe what Dolores knew to be something called Obesity Management. Imagine the humiliation if they did that to humans queuing at McDonald's or Burger King or Krispy Kreme Doughnut—do not!—stands!).

But what would I know about DNA, or cheetahs or pumas or ocelots or caracals for that matter? Or McDonald's etc? I am, after all, a cat. A sly and clever cat, it is true. A wily, calculating and very very beautiful cat. But a cat nonetheless. A housebound flat-cat. I have no access to the terminology of human science, although I am struggling to acquire some biped language: the sound *X*, for instance. *Eks*, pronounced in varying degrees of approval or offense, denotes a request for my presence or a condemnation of some recent and unwelcome action; reward or reprimand.

It is hard to discern the distinction because I have no access, either, to the human moral code.

I am required, rather, to be somehow inscrutable, occasionally affectionate, and most often indifferent to human blandishments, except when my stomach tells me that the giant bipeds who think they understand me must be persuaded to forage on my behalf and offer provender.

As a cat, I have impulses rather than detailed game plans, whose logic is not readily evident to the two-legged monsters I have acquired as my feeders, acolytes and servants. Or, indeed, to me.

Why, for instance, do I sometimes take it into my head, at a time in the dark hours when no food or company is forthcoming, to propel myself at speed down the long, central corridor of the biped lair, tossing myself into the air with giddy loop-the-loops and high-dive twists to land on the human sleep-pad with such force that lights go on and the word *eks* is pronounced by a voice I recognize to be both male and angry.

Why do I prowl across somnolent biped forms under

feathery covers, probing with my paws for the firm, warm terrain of certain mysterious zones of their bodies?

Are these the moments when they—humans, that is, not cats, of course—would prefer to be sleeping? How would I know? I have no real memory of my forebears. I was removed from my parents and siblings in my earliest days. I have lived since then in a moving forest of enormous legs many times my own height that end in a lower horizontal plane that could crush me—although that does not prevent me from trying to weave between them, potentially tripping them, sensing their presence through my whiskers, furry flanks and tail.

I have no quadruped contacts or acquaintances. I sometimes think I am turning into a biped or that some process is underway to confuse my felinity with the otherness of my companions. My life is full of such barely perceived musings that cross my consciousness like shadows and then are gone, leaving only an interrogative trace. Like the grin of the Cheshire Cat.

The what?

But why, despite my title as a flat-cat, with every known creature comfort of board and lodging, games, toys, catnip, regular meals, occasional "treats" resembling prawns (I know only that I like prawns, but I do not know what they are or do) would I plot and fret and try to position myself so that, when the bipeds fail to enforce the elaborate security precautions they undertake before opening the big white barrier leading to the universe beyond my immediate knowledge, I may propel myself at speed out into that space of heady liberation?

And why, oh why, do I choose, during these giddy

moments of freedom, to scamper upward, using the series of platforms that lead to other human boxes rather than down to where my instincts tell me there is access to the perils and delights of life beyond the cat flap—faint intimations of strange odors: leaf mold, urine, slugs, roots, traces of many other cats, pussies galore? (How do I even know how to describe these elements, other than by supposition about a world I have perceived through the hard, invisible, transparent barriers that enable me to sit for hours and follow the antics of flying, winged things, and loud rumbling large things and quadrupeds on leads that do not share my flat-cat ground rules? How can I prevent myself from inquiring into these mysteries, to the extent that I can? How can I know what curiosity did to the cat?)

My power of memory is of itself so capricious that I cannot recall what I truly remember and what I do not. But I believe there was an episode when the big white barrier of my prison opened for a long time and I sped and scuttled and headed uphill along the platforms and no biped pursued me and my hypersensitive ears detected the familiar sound of the barrier below closing. But I heard it from the outside! And I learned fear.

If I knew what Stockholm syndrome was, I would say I displayed it because, without my biped captors to recapture me, I had no real idea what to do, or really where I was, except that the urge that sends me usually to my dark litter box came upon me and I had no means of access to my private place so, perforce, was obliged to perform the intimate act in the liberated zone and, out of courtesy, did so outside another of the barriers in a higher place than my usual habitat. The cat, in other words, shat on the mat.

Then I detected the sound of the barrier below opening and voices crying, "X, X, X," in various tones of despair, wheedling and pleading. I scuttled down the same platforms as I had just ascended. I ignored the evidence of my presence deposited on a higher plane. And I allowed myself to be picked up and nuzzled and given an inexplicable treat—a reward I assumed, and who could blame me, for leaving my waste matter at a distant barrier rather than on my own doorstep, following, I believe, a human adage, and so resolved that, if ever I staged another breakout, I would do the same in the same place and thus qualify for another treat.

Well, you can't always be 100 percent right, even as a cat. My toilet functions drew some kind of response from an upper-floor biped. I was reprimanded, although, being a cat, I could not link the raised angry unpleasant voices to a specific event, or even to myself. And so, of course, the next time I escaped, I ventured to the same place intent on repeating my performance to earn a new reward. But before I could even begin to arrange myself, a great towering barrier swung open and, looking upward, I found myself peering over vast distances into the face of an unknown biped who looked down at me with an expression recognizable—even across the chasm of the species—as one of pure malice that injected a kind of pinky, purply hue into features distorted by rage. There was noise, confusion. A second unrecognized biped stood behind the first. Neither of them wore the wrappings favored by their kind. Both appeared to be of a gender I had once been. But these impressions had barely been registered before, with my heightened sense of terminal, imminent threat, I became aware of a raised, swinging thing—the humanoid equivalent of a paw—that was accelerating toward me, and so I was able to turn and flee before it connected. And, for once, my inner navigational systems ordered descent and before I knew it I was hurtling back into more familiar environs where identifiable bipeds tut-tutted and hoisted me to great altitude to stroke my stomach.

Human anger is not pleasant for small, vulnerable animals. Imagine if humans were shouted at by members of an alien species two hundred feet tall—they would soon understand why creatures develop bolt-holes between suitcases below sleep-pads, behind sofas near warmth, among the piles and layers of artificial skins the bipeds collect to adorn and shield themselves.

My preferred retreat is only occasionally available when accidental access is permitted to the large, crowded, dark spaces where humans put the body coverings they use as compensation for having no fur, and the barriers which are usually closed are left open.

("No animal shall wear clothes." Who said that? No, I don't mean *who said that* as in which human folding paper thing contained that question. I mean: who said that in my head? Is there someone else in here with me? Because the answer to the former question would be Orwell's pigs and I don't even know how I would begin to know that. And the latter question would worry me—if I knew how to fret. But if there was someone in here with me, they could perhaps explain things to me, like: what is an Orwell? Who is a pig?)

Reaching my favorite hiding place is an adventure in

its own right because the only way to get there is vertically with a leap and a bound and a scramble that propels you upward, past the three shiny knobs of the places where bipeds store items to disguise their pudgy paws and enormous, inelegant (mostly) unlicked bottoms and onto the places above where, if you don't fall, you can snuggle into the woolly, scented chest coverings and turn yourself around and look back onto the human sleep-pad and you can hear them calling, "X, X," and know from the growing anxiety of their tones that they do not know where you are and worry that you have somehow gotten past the great white barrier again and have left your calling card on a higher plane.

Again.

three

Dolores Tremayne found herself snooting and snuffling across the cork floor in the kitchen. In her human experience, the only time she could recall nostrils being put to comparable use was when associates at college or at work gatherings—flatmates, candidate lovers, high-flying executives before the inevitable fall—ingested lines of white powder, which she declined, in part out of fear of losing control to some chemical reaction and in part out of revulsion at the global trade in narcotics that ruined lives and diverted billions from state exchequers where they might be better spent on health care and schooling and other human requirements. But now her snoots and sniffles seemed reflexive rather than recreational, as if she was questing for something she could not immediately identify, like a person looking for a light switch in a darkened room, or programming a GPS while on the move in unknown, threatening neighborhoods.

She was not, of course, a person per se. She was, physically at least, a cat. Or at least she was a human in thrall to a cat, locked into a cat, as bonded to X as Nelson Mandela to his jailers on Robben Island, from which there was never any unplanned escape. The comparison had little relevance to her since she had no means of discourse, of negotiation with her captor. X—or Dolores within—would not be freed because the world demanded it at rock concerts, or threatened punishment unless the cage was unlocked. She did not even know whether X herself could hear her captive's *Cry Freedom*.

She navigated past a fragment of what her human mind knew to be a snapped-off corner of potato chip, but her feline appetites displayed no interest. (The Dolores in her fretted that the cleaning lady from the Philippines must have missed it and her family did not seem to care about this rodent-luring debris.) She moved on. She was not a dog, a canine vacuum cleaner devouring any fallen item. Cats had higher standards. She crossed the kitchen, navigating through an enormous arch that reminded her human side of the central cavity of the Arc de Triomphe. She crossed some light-colored material, amid blocks of seating arrangements for bipeds. At her level—and she knew this because it had been on her human mind for weeks—a tall mirror had been placed on its side along a skirting board until she and her husband agreed where to install it. Passing it now, she saw a faintly haughty creature—long-haired, slinky, sloe-eyed, blue-retinaed, endowed with a pelt of unique shadings: ivory, burnt umber, charcoal. Its face was dark and smoky, like a Venetian carnival mask against the lighter tones of its cranium and body. Its ears were almost black, set on either side of a wedge of pale fur extending from its blond spine. If you were human and had studied your kings and queens of England, a ruff of pure white around the neck would recall Elizabethan fashions.

The flanks were mottled with darker patches, like the markings of a parrot fish. Its paws were dark with silky hair between the pads, and its tail a great, gray brush that would outdo any fox.

That is me! That is what I have become. To be part of X, Dolores found herself thinking, was quite an honor. If she was a cat, then she was a superior version of the species.

Appropriately enough. In her human life, Dolores Tremayne was a powerhouse, indomitable, the embodiment of the new, female, formerly disadvantaged executive. She had overcome the stereotypes of race and gender, bursting through glass walls and ceilings, propelling herself upward with ballistic purpose. Like scientists at Mission Control, invested in her success and in awe of her celestial ascent, her family watched her zoom into the stratosphere then welcomed her back with her payload of promotions and bonuses and exotica from distant galaxies—ostrich eggs from Johannesburg; megapixel, multizoom HD-enabled cameras from Hong Kong; gold chains from Dubai; backgammon sets inlaid with mother-of-pearl from Beirut and Cairo; jade from Beijing; iPads from New York.

Her perfect achievement could not be measured purely in income, although that was satisfyingly substantial. She had given birth to two beautiful daughters. She financed the writerly ambitions of her deliciously sexy husband ("white British," according to the forms he filled out) who seemed happy enough to stay home and do the school run and supervise the staff in the hours of downtime between bouts of halting, anguished composition and the necessary displacement activities that nourish the creative soul.

His first novel—*Birth*—had been well received, if not well sold or marketed. He had a three-book contract, and she assumed that, in her absences, he was gestating the second of the trilogy. In the days of mechanical typewriters and A4 paper, she might have expected to see a slowly growing pile of completed script next to the clattering keys, like in that movie in the empty hotel with the famous actor and the boy and the woman. But that measure of progress had given way to the inscrutability of a hard drive and a backup USB stick, neither of which offered any clue to the work in progress.

She did not pry.

She was too busy to pry.

She did not ask to see his latest effort.

All work and no play.

The book. The movie. What was it called?

"All work and no play makes Jack a dull boy." That was all the fake author had written. Page after page of it. Volumes worthy in bulk of Tolstoy, but worth their weight only in paper, used paper at that. Paper soiled by fraudulent effort. But if you flipped the adage—all play and no work—what happened in Gerald's life? And with whom did he play?

REDRUM! Murder spelled backward. That was one of the linguistic tricks in the book. What does it take to drive a biped to that extreme sanction, to give someone a real redrummering?

Jack Nicholson. The star. No dull boy there, of course.

In secret, part of her calculated that provided Gerald looked after the girls—who adored having a long-haired, bohemian father whose brown-eyed gaze melted the hardest teacherly hearts, male or female, at parents' evening—then that was fine.

And another part thought that, as long as their separations ended in passionate coupling that seemed to have lost none of its multiple magic over the years, that was fine, too, a bonus, an affirmation that their relationship, built on absences rather than shared drudgery, enabled them to survive the advancing years that frayed the fabric of so many of her friends' marriages.

But another part of her frowned in puzzlement: the first novel had been published three years earlier. In a business that determined success or failure with unseemly haste, it had slipped into oblivion. He gave talks about the "craft of the novel" at obscure literary festivals, allowing tantalizing hints of his rough-diamond-northern-English accent to creep back into his voice, as if to suggest a life of deprivation and hardship at the lonesome coalface of composition. (Coalface had once been a possible alternative name for X, but had been considered far too literal. Possibly offensive.) The paperback of *Birth* would be stacked on a table for him to sign for those who purchased it—many of them, she had noticed at one gathering, quite comely young women. But, despite his promotional efforts, his wit, his charm, his slick manipulation of audiences, his Amazon ranking seemed like a mathematical impossibility: were there really 3,780,922 books that were better loved than his? He had extended and re-extended the delivery date for the second of the trilogy—*Marriage*—and the slow pace of the artistic endeavor gave her cause to worry whether it was not only the title but also their eponymous civil state that was holding him back from realizing what the kinder reviewers had called the promise of his debut oeuvre.

The third volume—*Death*—seemed far-distant and she prayed that it would become a reality before life, or, in this case, its termination, came to imitate art.

The Shining. That was the name of the film. And the book. Stephen King the author.

Had Stephen King ever seen a single word of his placed at 3,780,923 on the lists? Doubtful.

No longer snooting, X has determined that it is time to patrol the perimeters of her domain. X saunters down the long central corridor.

Sit back. Enjoy the ride.

They are in the guest bedroom now, she and X.

I spring upward from the carpet. The sleep-pad feels unpleasantly soft with no biped bumps and bones to guide my paws. No temperature spikes to draw my heat-seeking explorations. No sound of breath, grunts, whimpers, snores.

The sleep-pad is empty. There is no immediate danger but, as a cat, I know how easily that can change. Part of the whiteness has been folded back, so there is a soft, yielding ridge, then a smooth plain, then the mountain range called Pillows. Next to the sleep-pad, the humans keep containers and artificial suns that they control in their biped way, turning day into night, night into day, conjuring giddy images from darkened picture boxes.

There is a silvery, slidy square of something alien that I flip with my paw.

It falls from its place on a flat area below the artificial sun. I push it hither and thither. It is not terribly interesting. There is no purchase for a sharp, extended claw. It does not squeal or take flight. It has no tail or fur and holds no promise of sustenance. I bat it back and forth a bit but it does not seem to want to play. I sniff it. Neutral. Shades of chemical. Notes of lubricant. Unpleasant but inspiring curiosity.

I take it between my sharp little teeth. Its texture is difficult to place in my catalogue of sensations: hard, metallic on the outside, but something softer seems hidden within, bouncy, like one of those toys with which the humans try to distract me. My incisor easily penetrates the outer casing but the interior is glutinous, repellent. I bite a little deeper.

An unpleasant taste. Slimy. A voice inside me is telling me what it is but I cannot quite decipher it. And whose voice would it be anyhow?

The sound of the great white barrier opening and closing alarms us.

Redrum most foul may be afoot. For all we know or care.

We flatten ourselves—X and I—and turn, surveying options. Unusually, the access gates to the warm storage zones are open, welcoming. Dolores tries to say something, but she has no voice and no one is listening anyhow.

They traverse the sleep-pad. Leopard crawl, she thinks; but how would a cat know to attach that label to its reflexive, hunter's advance, however appropriate to the action it described?

They leap down from the sleep-pad, bound across open space, accelerate, gather strength in powerful rear legs, and without thinking launch vertically into the place where bipeds store spare skins and coverings; past the lower part with the shiny knobs; carried upward with enormous, thrusting power; scrambling for a toe-hold, claw-hold, paw-hold, bringing up the rear legs to grapple for vertical progression, shooting improbably past what Dolores recognizes as shelves of agnès b. blouses, folded Armani jeans, cashmere from Brora, Ralph Lauren polos.

I am in among the warm, comforting things that smell somehow familiar, associated with a person who has left my life—her work fatigues, her camouflage. I turn in this dark, narrow space. I settle on my haunches, my left front paw folded under me, the right paw jutting out like a stump.

My acute aural capabilities signal approaching human voices, one on a higher register, the other lower, more familiar, the one that makes my name a threat: "X, X, X! What have you done now?"

My vibrissae that humans call whiskers have established my ability to fit in the space between yielding, warm piles. Framed by the limits of my adopted environment, I feel safe, although from another perspective I am trapped because there is no rear exit. I cannot leave my hiding place without forfeiting my invisibility.

The barriers close but not completely. There is a splinter, a shard of vision. I want to flee but something holds me back. I look around, sensing that somehow I am not alone, but there is no one here with me that I can see. Unlike the events I—we—can see unfolding through the crack between the doors.

four

With unblinking cat's eyes, Dolores Tremayne is watching her all-too-human husband and her all-too-human neighbor outside whose front door X once defecated. She wishes to turn away but X does not. She does not wish to see them removing their clothes in haste, but X is indifferent to her sentiments. The sight of the female nakedness is oddly familiar. It recalls some hazardous event that reduced her stock of lives to eight. A jumble of ghostly memories. Upstairs, downstairs. In short order. In panic.

There is some giggling. Her husband, the novelist Gerald Tremayne, is popping a rolled-up banknote and a small, folded package into a drawer in the nightstand on his side of the guest bed and retrieving a small, silver, square wrapper from the carpet where X or I flipped it. He places it in the drawer.

At least it is the guest bedroom. Is there some comfort in that? Probably not. Dolores has more powerful systems of recall than X. She knows what she is watching. She can identify the players. She wants to cry out, cry foul, but cannot. It is as if a rusting dagger, plucked from some slimy mire, dripping with rot and infection, has been plunged into her heart. Every twist and turn of the blade chokes her, compounds her anguish, introduces fresh toxins into those rapid-fire questions. Why? How long? Who else?

Her husband is displaying a degree of tumescence. His companion expresses approval, fiddles with her nose, emitting a not-very-ladylike snorting noise. And he swore he was clean! Goddammit, I paid for that fancy nose-candy because his publisher's advance reached the end of its very brief financially viable life months ago.

So that's where his allowance is going—financing the gradual erosion of his septum. She must have been mad not to see it. Mad in the sense of craziness, defined as repeating the same error over and over again in the expectation of a different outcome. He had been into drugs when they met—albeit as a purveyor to her college cohort—and now he was back to his old ways. She felt a stirring of liberal guilt—obviously not the same stirring as consumed the entangled bipeds in her line of vision. Could you typecast people like that? Profile them? She did not approve of racial profiling in her own doings. So why stigmatize lying, cheating, northern, sleazebag cokeheads? Unless there were circumstances to confirm the stereotypes, the incontrovertible evidence of genetic determinism. Like the scene before her.

The defense rests, m'lud. A crime of passion. Redrum. A marriage redrummed by heinous betrayal. For innocence read foolishness, blindness, self-deception.

She feels X wriggle uncomfortably. X was physically

spayed after her first heat when she alarmed the girls by shedding her cuddly kitten persona to become a sex-driven demon, desperate and available. She has gotten a little chunkier since her operation but is still essentially playful. She is available to chase feathers on sticks, leap at Christmas wrappings, climb into small cardboard boxes as if they were her private bunkers, but not to mate or procreate. Yet, some vestigial trace of feline passion seems to be rekindled by what she can see through the not-quite-closed doors, this not-quite-cliché: husband and neighbor, rumbled by a voyeuristic cat providing much the same services as a private eye employed by a suspicious spouse.

A private cat's eye, stirred by an ancient longing. A sleuth denied the ability to report her findings. X and Dolores: investigator and client. All in one. Vaguely, X recognizes the naked female foot that had once swung at her with lethal intent. Specifically, Dolores recognizes the upstairs neighbor.

You can cut out the anatomy of estrus, Dolores is thinking, but you can never quite quell the urge. It is a lesson that age will bring to us all. But not yet. Not in her household. Not for her husband.

It is like watching a dream trainwreck of the carriage in which you are traveling: horrifying and fascinating. Tables lurch and crash. Suitcases fly from the racks as if on a spacecraft. Drinks bottles, cups, saucers assume ballistic qualities. You watch your own destruction. The familiar planes—vertical, horizontal—warp and bulge and turn topsy-turvy. You watch your life to date, and the assumptions that hold it in place, simply disintegrating.

There is nothing beyond the gross breach of trust, of faith.

Reluctantly, wishing she hadn't, Dolores remembers the day her upstairs neighbor telephoned down to them after one of X's occasional forays onto the staircase.

The neighbor—Jenny Steinem—is angry. Since her flatmate left, she lives alone, right above them. Sometimes, usually on rainy evenings when jogging is not an option, she skips on a rope for exercise. She is a mere wisp of a person—as Dolores can see all too clearly from her vantage point in her wardrobe: the androgynous bottom, the pubic fluff and prison-camp hip bones. But when she skips, the thump resonates through the bedroom ceiling as if she is having percussive sex with a very energetic lover, as she did before her partner left.

That, evidently, is where Dolores miscalculated in the never-ending assessment of threat and opportunity that governs so many interpersonal apartment house relationships—staircase alliances, balcony feuds, campaigns fought over parked bicycles and incontinent pets, screeching parrots, over-loud infatuation with Led Zeppelin or Wagner's Ring Cycle. Jenny's partner was called Waltraud and came from Baden-Württemberg. They had seemed an item that could only be replaced by reference to identical gender. The apparent monosexuality of the neighbor's inclinations had, Dolores now thinks, lulled her into a false sense of security. Vis-à-vis Gerald, that is. The upstairs neighbor had never put a move on her. Or the girls. And was unlikely to see her desires fulfilled by one so male as her husband. She had assumed.

But Jenny seems, indubitably, to swing both ways and

silly, naïve, deceived Dolores had not included that possibility in her calculations.

After X's indiscretion on the mat outside Jenny's door, Dolores had answered the phone. A Californian-accented voice screeched at her.

"Your cat has shat on my doorstep! SHAT!"

Dolores is full of apology. She is on neighborly, first-name terms with the woman upstairs but they are not close. Personally, she believes that a little cat poop is a fair reward for hours of skipping and thumping and obsessive attention to burning off calories and exploring the aural frontiers of the libido. But she hears herself saying: "Jenny, I'm terribly sorry. Really. I'll ask Gerry to pop up and clean."

"Please do," says Jenny and hangs up abruptly.

Dolores remembers how Gerald Tremayne left the family apartment armed with a dustpan, rubber gloves, carpet shampoo and two Tesco plastic bags for the evidence.

X was nowhere to be seen, of course. Being a cat she had divined the moment to disappear.

When he returned—after spending longer, in retrospect, than anyone needed to be absent on such a simple mission—he had a smile on his face. And Dolores remembers his words.

"Well, I think I calmed her down."

That is not what he is doing now.

Watching her husband, part of her feels detached. It is her feline part, switched off to human antics: so lacking in animal grace compared to a cat's suppleness, its sense of cool.

Another part is appalled.

Please, she is thinking, do not do our special things. Do not do those things with mouth and tongue and protuberance and bodily cavity which I had never previously experienced. Please do not show that I was merely a foil for your skillful repertoire, like the magician's stage sidekick, present merely to be bisected and then to stand aside, deflecting applause to the supremo of spells and wizardry.

She wants to shout, or somehow say something, anything to stop it. Like those TV viewers who do not wish to see the result of a sporting fixture, she wants X to look away NOW. And failing that, she wants action. Kinetic action. The disruption of infidelity by any means.

A loud miaow to distract them, for instance. She wants X to leap forth, claws bared, and dig them into that scrawny rump athwart her husband, riding him like a demented jockey in the final furlong. She wants the cat that contains her mind or soul to intrude, break cover, run amok among the mementoes stored in the guest room—a royal wedding mug showing Charles and Diana, a framed photograph of his parents long ago before their separation, a winner's cup from a children's contest at a forgotten ski resort. She wants their combined being to hurtle along the shelves, sending porcelain and silverware flying and crashing.

But X may have other calculations.

Gerald has never really liked X. When they met, he called himself a dog person—ever since his father walked the whippet to the pigeon loft above the slag-heaps, if only in the cinematic self-image he had chosen to express his quintessential alienation as a northerner in the perfidious south. Who knows if there was ever a dog, a bird, an industrial landscape borrowed from L. S. Lowry? Why would the great novelist invent lives only on his laptop?

Besides, X knows from her previous experience with the flying female foot, retribution might be swift and terminal. And anyhow, X seems content to let the nightmare unfold, like some perverse reversal of one of those lewd shows Dolores had heard about in the red light districts of Hamburg or Amsterdam where humans watch animals entwine bestially.

After some preliminaries, during which the neighborly Jenny offers some oral encouragement to the husbandly arousal, they grapple themselves under the covers so that all a cat can see is a billowing mound of sheet and duvet, an occasional foot—*that* foot—protruding temptingly as if a game of nibble-the-toe, invented during her kitten-hood, is being offered.

Dolores can decipher the way things are going, like one of those choreographed encounters in televised wrestling bouts where the mandatory procession of headlocks and forearm smashes must unfold before the declaration of victory. The woman is rocking back and forth, buttocks clenched. Then the protagonists regroup and she is on her back, legs akimbo to judge from the shape of the expensive bedding. (Selected and paid for by—yes—Dolores. From—yes—John Lewis. Again. Saturdays at the Brent Cross Shopping Centre. With the mad hordes, the locust swarms of shoppers consuming iPhones and handbags and shirts and trousers and dresses and blue jeans and crystal glasses and curtains. And stuff from

Boots the chemist: shampoo. Condoms. She buys them, too. French ones in their shiny silver packaging. Prophylaxis now destined for a familiar function in a different, dark environment from the one intended—a very small mercy, indeed.)

A hand reaches out from the mountains of percale cotton and goose down. It fumbles around in the bedside drawer.

Another line? Already?

Gerald reaches for the square silver wrapper. Dolores cannot see, with X's somewhat unfocused feline vision, if it is the same square silver wrapper that she—or X— chose to puncture.

Her acute hearing detects noises suggesting that the upstairs neighbor is in some kind of dire pain that lingers and rises and falls. Gerald does not inspect the wrapper. He tears it. His hand withdraws under the bespoke covers, holding the slippery, lubricated contents, as if transferring an oyster from its glistening shell. There is some new wriggling.

Not long now, Dolores figures from experience. The noise switches from female tones of submission and need and fulfilment to male grunts; breath heaving like in the last hundred yards of the half-marathon that time she trained and ran for charity and advancement in the firm and her daughters praised her and thought she was crazy, wonderfully so.

Climax almost operatic. On both sides. The scrawny diva sings. Pavarotti-husband modulates an ascending crescendo.

Think Puccini. *Turandot*. No one, certainly, is sleeping here.

Vincerò!

Though for every great victory, there is a bitter defeat.

Of course the neighbor won't hear through the ceiling because the neighbor is belowdecks, pinioned, audience and participant, stimulant and receptacle, repository of the vanities. Silence. That moment. The final curtain. The stunned auditorium. Murmurs of mutual congratulation, amazement.

Bravo! Brava!

The drooping ovation. The coital claque.

Please don't say it was better.

"It was the best. Ever."

It is muffled but she hears it. The final betrayal.

Now, she believes, there will be those few moments he is so good at, the warm descent from the golden uplands, the assurance, the verbal sugarcoating on the raw physicality of the act. Whispers. Strokes. Hugs. If her husband ever took a real job, it would be in a call center, soothing bruised and cheated egos; or in some airport control tower, talking down the stricken airliner. Assuring. Confident. Knowing.

But her cat's ears detect a shift in emphasis. Something has loosened in the coda of mutual congratulation.

Complaint. Questioning. Strident tones like after the poop incident. The pink-purple face. The indignant rage.

A single piercing wail that a cat would recognize as a signal of acute alarm, mortal hazard.

X's wide-angle eyes see the Californian woman leap

from the snow fields of bedding and run to the "family" bathroom. Clutching at the damp tuft between her glistening upper thighs.

Sounds now of running liquid. As in the biped water box.

Furtively, Gerald reaches to the bedside where he had casually dropped the floppy, knotted tube of stretched, extended latex. Even with a cat's eyes, at this range, you can see the great gash in the tip of it, the shredding, the evidence of catastrophic failure.

There is not a trace of his usually abundant and perilously fecund deposit in this bank of love. There is no talking down from this cataclysm. No flaps and air brakes and reverse thrust to coax the stricken jetliner to the runway's haven, forestalling certain disaster. This is not a night at the movies. Or reality TV. This is the daytime of real reality. The howling descent. Gravity's triumph. "Brace! Brace!" the flight crew bellows. But everyone knows it is ending in tears. Not *Vincerò*, after all. Think *Richard III* or *Macbeth* or *Hamlet*. Strewn bodies. Hubris leading to the fall, the plummet of destiny.

Gerald is inspecting the bright silver square. You can see the mental gears grind, the cognitive cogs turn.

Sabotage! His condom has been sabotaged. By a sharp, single, needlepoint incision, slender as a stiletto. Like a cat's tooth.

This is not the moment for X to break cover.

So she does.

five

Scamper away from the guest room. A fast turn worthy of Lewis Hamilton at the cavernous litter box—a fecal Aladdin's cave—into the central corridor.

Reckless speed now. Claws finding purchase in the expensive sea-grass carpeting chosen for its durability from a specialist store in Belsize Park. Or was it Hampstead? Or Notting Hill?

Breakneck maneuvers. A door opens. X propels herself between the spindly, dripping, towel-draped legs of the upstairs neighbor emerging from the bathroom.

My bathroom. Our family bathroom.

Almost tangling them. Fresh shrieks of alarm.

"That fucking cat."

A swinging dainty foot that almost connects, like a World Cup soccer tackle provoking a dive and anguished, aggrieved appeal. The foot. That same lethal appendage to the biped leg. Discount the threat, the memory. Speed is all. No time now for theatrics. Survival is at stake.

Her husband is calling, but X understands with instinctive clarity that this call must be ignored. It is full of rage. Madness.

Carried along in pell-mell flight, Dolores cannot fault the feline logic. Because she is not herself. She cannot, as her instincts would like, stand up to him, fight her corner, condemn, assail, express her betrayal, denounce his treachery with tears and shouts and slaps and beating with bunched angry fists. She cannot call a lawyer or a counselor or a hit man. Or even expel the treacherous, scheming neighbor. For she is a cat carrying the spirit, the essence of a woman whose soul has been cut to the quick.

In human terms, they—she and X—are admitting their knowledge of his guilt by fleeing, and their own guilt as voyeurs. They are outgunned, exposed to an overwhelming physical superiority. They are lightly armed guerrilla forces, darting through the undergrowth. He is a one-man napalm strike desperate to happen; the neighbor, a drone-fired cruise missile of pure malice needing only the press of the button.

The anger in the novelist's voice persuades her that they must take refuge from rage.

So, thankfully, must he.

"What the hell? I mean. How could you? How could you be so careless?"

X has found Portia's bedroom with its strip of police crime scene tape, left over from a burglary attempt, across the teenager's door. It is slightly ajar. Enough for a snout to push wide enough until the vibrissae signal an adequate pathway for the fluffy, cozy, now quivering body.

Through X, Dolores experiences fear as she has never felt it before. Absolute. Visceral. Reflexive. Beyond reason.

X has grown up with no knowledge of threat. If she were allowed outside, how would she know that, while four legs are good, four wheels are bad; that sly Reynard the Fox would snap her neck with one flick of his or her jaws; that the world is so much more than three squares a day and a surfeit of cuddles?

Does she know anything that is red in tooth and claw?

Except her husband's paramour.

"Never mind the damned cat. What about me? I could be pregnant?" Her voice rises interrogatively at the end of the sentence. The word fills the moment with universal horror.

"Pregnant?" A word not welcome in the lothario lexicon.

"Yes. Fucking pregnant. Which part of the word do you not understand?"

X tunnels. Under the bed.

Between plastic storage containers of sheet music and snowsuits and discarded dolls from earlier years there is a tunnel, a maze, leading to a secret silent core, like that inner sanctum in the Great Pyramid of Giza.

The what?

Pray we do not need the litter box, Dolores is thinking. Pray curiosity does not lure us forth to kill the cat, as Gerald surely would.

Knowing what he suspects.

The incisor piercing of the condom.

Exhibit A.

Anthropomorphization of the incident: as if a malignant human had plotted his downfall, lurking beyond the arras to conspire.

Biped voices in the long corridor. Dolores guesses that they are discussing cycles of fertility, phases between menstrual periods, the probability of disaster, abortion.

"What if I don't want to get rid of it?" her neighbor is saying.

And, quite abruptly, she understands that if she had not awoken as a cat, she would not have known what was going on in her own home during her frequent professional absences. Cats learn many things that humans would never suspect, but they do not always remember them. They cannot testify or take action. They feel no obligation, indeed have no ability, to confess or bear witness. But humans condemned to a cat's life know and understand all. Except how they got there. And how they will get out of it to wreak vengeance.

"Listen, lover boy. It's either me or the cat. Your choice." Lady Macbeth. Out, damned cat, out, I say.

Foul whisperings are abroad: unnatural deeds do breed unnatural troubles. Dolores recalls the final year at high school, in the amateur dramatics society. A walk-on part. Gentlewoman. Act 5 Scene 1. Good night, good doctor. The final curtain call before the trek north to uni. And the doomed tryst so much later with Gerald Tremayne. So often postponed that it might not have happened. There would have been others. There were others. But not since Gerald. The folly of fidelity.

"Heaven knows what she has known," the gentle-woman says. And now I know, too.

X and Dolores hear the big white barrier bang closed. They hear the footsteps returning to the guest room and, soon afterward, they hear a rumbling sound that Dolores knows to be the washing machine sluicing out the damned spot. And the garbage bin opening and closing. Toilet flushing.

Cleanup. Cover-up. Before the domestic lady arrives with her Tagalog cell phone banter and sharp eyes for anomalies, stains, creases in sheets that should be pristine on beds that are supposed to be unused, in reserve for guests.

Another sound. A box of treats being rattled.

X stirs, settles. Dolores feels her pulling back, with-drawing into the hiding place no human can enter without tearing aside the storage boxes, excavating Portia's past, the palimpsest of early youth, her blossoming.

A light now, in a white color range. The predator stalking. Torch in hand. Light turning milky, diffused through the opaque plastic, playing over shapes, memories: Barbie, Furby, My Little Pony, half the contents of Hamleys and F.A.O. Schwarz, Knopf Im Ohr. Portia's first drawing. "For Mummy" in uncertain script. Primary colors and great bold daubs. Yellow sun. Cerulean sky. The green, green grass of home.

A new approach, conciliatory, wheedling. Fooling no one.

"Pretty pussy."

"Treaty-wheaties."

"No one's cross with you, X."

"Good cat!"

Another sound. Ding-a-ling. Familiar.

"Hi, baby. How's my girl?"

Portia? Astra? Gerald has answered his telephone and stands up.

The darkness returns. X breathes very lightly, inaudible even to feline ears.

Sound of incoming electronic voice. Welcome, familiar. Portia. The elder, who sneaks prawn treats for X, and flips her on her back, and rubs the deep gray thatch of her cashmere-soft belly.

"Now? Sure. Be right there."

More voice scrambled by the miniaturized speaker in the top-of-the-line smartphone.

"Both of you? Fine. No worries. No. Not busy at all. Finished for the day."

And how! I wonder if he is aware of the cruel irony of that last remark. Then his voice takes on a harder edge.

"It's not over, X. Wherever you are. Not by a long chalk. Not by the hair on your chinny-chin-chin."

So now she is a pig? And he will blow the house down? Come home. Dolores. Come home.

But I am home. I am here. I have seen all. And can tell no one.

What did I do? Did I not nurture him, pander to his bedtime foibles, praise his talents, stroke the writerly ego and its physical appendage? Was it my job? The absences? The girls? The home-husbandry? Did I neglect, or dis, or otherwise importune the genius?

Is it because I is black? An Ali G voice.

Oh my God. I have never thought that before.

She has not thought that before because she has not wanted to. Because she has never wished to see disadvantage in her lineage.

It is like one of those moments at the movies when the focus shifts from whatever is in the foreground, making it blurred and indistinct while the background snaps into crystalline view, invisible until that moment but now revealed, illuminating what was always there but not always seen.

Dolores thinks of her parents—one African, one English. Her father is from the southern quadrant of the continent, a hero of liberation yet steeped in the acquired culture of exile in Britain, her mother's native land. People who know him only from telephone conversations sometimes make racial assumptions based on his Oxbridge tones and his facility with quotations from Shakespeare. They are surprised, when they first meet him, to discover that he is equally fluent in Marx and Fanon—the prophets of the oppressed—and that his expressive canon ranges from the Nguni tongues of his distant past to a diplomat's ease with French and a smattering of conversational Russian from the days at Patrice Lumumba University in Moscow, the finishing school of the struggle.

Her father has tutored her from an early age in the premises of the Freedom Charter. She is a proud African, a product of his triumph over prejudice. Equality is her birthright. He has overcome, and so must she.

By upbringing, she has acquired an easy familiarity with the cosmopolitan idiom of dual citizenship and twin passports. Her mother, less polemical than her father, but equally committed to their shared principles, has nudged and coaxed her along a straight and narrow path of scholarly achievement, the new weapons in the new struggle against the divisions of class and color. Her daughter will suffer neither the slings of colonialism nor the arrows of humiliation that haunt her mother's memories of the bleak mill towns of Lancashire, the neglected heartland of blue-collar Britain where people lived shorter more stunted lives and left school early to play hands dealt from the bottom of the pack. And people from other places looked down on them and mocked them and made them the butt of cruel jokes.

Between them, her parents had proudly concluded, they had raised a daughter, an only child as it happened, who fused the best of both of them. Dolores has sought to pass on that same belief—veneer, perhaps—to her own daughters, ignoring the whispered asides of the soccer moms outside the fee-paying school where she has enrolled them to acquire even stronger shields of knowledge and polish and achievement. But she is not in denial about their difference; about the offhand malice of other children who have absorbed their parents' kitchen-table racial attitudes by osmosis; about the uneasy sense that, whether at home in London or on vacation in far-flung Africa, they are never really gifted with easy acceptance. They are outsiders wherever they finish up and have had to learn to stand their ground, to ignore the slights and barbs and lewd remarks. To say: this is me and I bow the knee to no one.

But now a vision of betrayal through the eyes of a cat had begun to unpick the assumptions.

Is it because I is black? Or not black enough?

Is it because I is a cat with a woman inside me, neither one thing nor wholly the other?

The faux-soccer, mock-hockey dad rattles keys, double-locks vestibule doors that prevent X from escaping onto the staircase outside the family apartment with its nooks and crannies and hiding places and favored spots for surreptitious pooping to acquire rewards.

My remarkable cat's ears detect him bounding down the stairs. My human memory conjures him forth, with his long, novelist's hair bouncing and his eyes gleaming, relishing the pretext to reverse the navy blue Range Rover Sport—mine on the ownership and insurance papers—from the garage and spin round to the fee-paying school where the girls receive their education and perform after-hours sport, save when the weather forces postponements and cancellations without refunds. As per contractual arrangement. Like today. Mercifully.

He will pull up and the other child-duty spouses will welcome him in the jumble of overpriced, overpowered SUVs in the parking lot, wondering, perhaps, why any woman would leave a hunk like that at home and go off traveling for work when all kinds of temptation might cross his loping path. And a black woman at that, their eyes will say, though their tongues are more discreet.

Over time, as the semesters have notched up, and the exorbitant fees with them, he has established first-name bonds with many of his fellow parents. At first he recognized them mainly by their late-model chariots, marveling sometimes at the wealth reflected in all those Porsche

Cayennes and Volvo XC90s and Mercedes ML350s. But then, as nodded greetings gave way to cautious introductions, he began to distinguish between them. Recognition by type—matronly, mature, trophy—led to first names. A social subgroup, bound by the shared experience of agendas set to educational rhythms, book-ended by the school bell and the sports ground. He was the only male among them, the fox in the chicken coop, the wolf in writerly clothing. Gerald. Call me Gerry. The familiar cast clustered around their charges. Rosemary, with the dogs and daughters, in her Mercedes Estate; Carmel, with the twinkly eyes in the big Audi Q7, with one child of her own and two by her spouse's previous relationship, prior to being smitten by her, lured and ensnared; Carlotta, just starting out, husband in the city, one child in prep, wondering when it would be her turn again to disappear for days and nights into Canary Wharf to win the bread. And what did they all think of him? Kept man? Stud? What did they think of his after-hours secrets, his nocturnal trespass across the frontiers of skin color? Did that, in fact, make them more curious about, or more fearful of, the chromatic reach of his sexuality? Did they, for one moment, imagine his childhood days, traipsing in worn sneakers to and from the local comprehensive school in a place so far north that they would imagine it shared latitudes with Reykjavík and Anchorage?

No SUVs there, back in the day. No waiting mums in his childhood world of errant, absent dads and zero-hour contract jobs and food banks and bare-knuckle contests for turf and dominion. And if they had known, would they have wondered how he had gotten here, infiltrating these leafy environs, the tribal traces of the north well-hidden, save for the vestigial lapses, the vocal contortions that betrayed the roots, affecting a kind of cosmopolitanism like an ill-fitting suit. Rosemary and Carmel and Carlotta would probably find his distant heritage vaguely exotic, heavy with literary antecedents. Oliver Mellors. Gabriel Oak. Laurel and Hardy. Bathsheba. Mixed with the mysteries of Africa.

But, when he meets their husbands—Toby and Christian and Dominic and Algie, old chap—he knows that they know what they all know: no amount of automotive ostentation can ever erase the codes of speech and vowel and consonant that bind Britons into their upbringings and locate them in the firmament of their appropriate class and status as surely as any GPS. You can take the boy out of Newcastle . . .

In all probability, the menfolk would not know with any certainty or exactitude the difference between Leeds and Manchester and Liverpool and Doncaster and Sunderland, except from the highway road signs or railroad name-boards as they speed north to grouse moors and salmon rivers and hunting-shooting-fishing weekends in tweeds and big private houses. But they understood that, when you saw those names, you drove on. Here be dragons. Here be crime, violence, drugs, housing projects, terminal hazard, menace signaled by flat vowels and flat caps, post-industrial moonscapes of derelict mills and Poundstretcher stores. In these places people would strip you of everything you had, out of spite and greed and envy and want, with none of the insouciance and finesse of the hedge-fund husbands and stock-option spouses who achieved the same effect on gullible investors with comparable avarice. Only the tactics were different.

No matter if people like that finished up in the parking lot of posh, private schools in North London, sliding their rock-star arses across the cream leather seats of their wives' Range Rovers. They still hailed from that lower order, across an unbridgeable void, direct descendants of highwaymen and brawlers and brigands of old who would not rest until the unearned wealth of the upper crust was transferred to their own, equally unsalaried coffers. As Honoré de Balzac wrote, all great fortunes sprang from great crimes.

And the same, theoretically, should be true in reverse: all great fortunes may be reversed by great crimes, although they rarely are. As every convicted cat burglar and unmasked Ponzi schemer knows to his or her everlasting regret.

When Gerald Tremayne heard their braying, drawling tones—the anthem of private schools and tuxedoed college dining clubs, and internships that led to gilt-edged futures—he knew that he would never gain access to the codebooks and signals charts by which they communicated. The references to Glyndebourne; the talk of fagging and scouts and bedders; the bespoke suits from the right tailors; Barbour jackets that never seemed to have been new, worn to a shine, steeped in the essence of wet gun-dog and misty moorland and fluttering, stricken pheasant. He understood that he stood forever apart from these men, though not necessarily from their wives.

six

He has brought them home. Portia, the firstborn, and Astra, two years her junior. X distinguishes between them because it is the elder biped who transmits the warmest signals while the younger seems prepared to cede primacy in the feline heart to her elder sister, caught between her seasons, kitten and cat, where veterinary intervention has frozen X forever. Portia is her soul mate. Astrid is like a sometimes-seen cousin. Portia loves X.

Once, she heard Astra ask her father whether she could have a puppy. Whatever that is.

I humor Portia, of course, because I know she likes to play and needs only a little coaxing from her innate shyness. In my tiny but powerful jaws, I bring her favorite toys to her. She likes simple things—a silver star on a strand of stretchy stuff, a round thing made of some bright orange material that I once saw wrapped around human energy food. She needs a little persuasion but I know she wants to overcome her modesty, her natural reticence.

(I hear these words and wonder if some other animal is speaking them from deep within me.)

So I perform a few predictable maneuvers to draw her out of her reluctance and help her find her happy side.

I jump. I sprint. I excel in catobatics worthy of the Olympiad, twisting in midair, landing on all four paws. And finally she is coaxed into the game. She tosses the bright sphere and I run after it to encourage her. She flicks the silvery star aloft and I leap. Silver is my favorite color. I am fascinated by silver. Between my teeth.

The thought stirs in my recent memory, like a zephyr through fallen leaves. (Again, I take exception to this simile as I am a flat-cat and have no direct knowledge of leaves, or zephyrs—for heaven's sake—except from what I can observe through the invisible barriers of my prison, my Robben Island. My what?)

Recent memory is a jumble of signals. Alarm. Danger. Threat. Something has happened that changes the harmony of my environment. There has been a shift, an injection of hostility. No. More than that. An infusion of peril. Life threatening. But what was it?

Bipeds love shiny surfaces as much as cats love silver. They spend endless hours staring at flat, smooth tablets, interrogating them, demanding that they yield up secrets from sleek, glossy surfaces that they stroke lovingly to conjure colors, shapes, configurations.

Cats are accused of endless indolence. But bipeds have produced their own pretexts to while away the hours on a much grander scale, invoking time-saving technology to fritter time itself. With my own eyes I have witnessed the birth of their inventions, arriving in huge coverings, mounted vertically on walls—portals into a captured world of colors and shapes, spheroids and ovals pursued by humans in standardized clothing. Sometimes in this parallel world that can be summoned and extinguished at will, there are quadrupeds whose cycles of death and pro-creation are explained by a wrinkled form of biped known as *National Treasure*. Look, X, I hear them say—snakes in packs, urban leopards, fellow felines far away. I track these apparitions at close quarters, stirred somehow by the quiver of a wing or whisker whose function is a mystery to me but whose observation makes my claws curl in antici-pation.

With the junior daughter at her side, the midrange bi-ped is stroking one of her toys, laid flat on the floor. It is of little immediate interest. It does not bounce, sparkle, offer a hint of taste, movement. It cannot be sniffed or consumed or chased or tortured. It is an inert object that does not cross my radar of the familiar.

She touches part of the toy and a sound emerges.

She takes my paw and lays it on the same part of the surface and the same sound emerges. Then she strokes another part and a different sound. I allow her to take my front paw again.

I do not at first attempt to scratch the shining surface. I follow her signals. I prod my stubby stump of a fist at different spaces on the shiny surface and chime-like sounds follow one another. The junior and midrange bipeds slap their large, clawless, furless, bony paws together and utter gurgly sounds that suggest contentment.

I have made them happy. Mission accomplished: humans do not know what they are seeking until they are placed clearly and unequivocally in front of it. And yet they consider themselves infinitely superior.

The junior and midrange bipeds touch the shiny surface in a different way and the monochrome bars disappear and other shapes emerge. They are the shapes of mice, which cats despise and wish to taunt into unpleasant, messy deaths. But how is this knowledge accessible to a tame creature such as I? I have never seen a mouse. I do not know what a mouse is for. But if I smelled one I would chase it. Is this something locked in me that I can never escape? Am I doomed to pursue animals I have never seen because my forebears, presumably, at some point did? And if so, is my whole life determined in advance, programmed as surely as these tablets—a series of stimuli and responses dictated by a past that can never be modified or altered or erased, no matter how hard I try to shake off history by molding and breeding a new persona?

Is it, in other words, because I is a cat?

And if I is a cat, what place do these human musings have in my lexicon?

My claws tap against the shiny surface. And the shapes keep coming so that I can attack them. But, no matter how much I spear and wound them, the shapes do not bleed. They offer no prospect of nourishment and show no sign of mortality. They make no sound. They do not squeal with that tiny, tinny agony expected of rodents in extremis, which I know to exist without ever having heard it. They are not real. I have been duped into responding, reflexively, to chimera.

I walk away, my tail high and mighty. I was never really interested in this frippery, this tedious interface masquerading as a real game played with feathers on sticks, golden balls.

Because I *is* a cat I is able to display insouciance in the face of indignity, going about my business as if I had never even thought of doing anything else. But they know I will be back.

seven

Have they done this on purpose, her clever, beloved daughters? Have they signaled through this game that she has a chance of communication?

They got X to play cat games on their tablet computer and, of course, as could be expected, X was brilliant, playing songs, chasing mice, responding to signals with appropriate zeal and intelligence. But Dolores glimpsed or sensed something else: the gaudy palette known as the desktop, the whole array of things that she used to know as apps but which are now just a jumble of shapes and patterns.

One of those patterns, those building bricks of biped cleverness, must permit communication. One of them must allow her to tell herself to come back before the home fires consume that which they are supposed to nurture. But which shape will unlock the door?

And when will her daughters leave their precious tablets lying around so that she can experiment, prise open the codes?

And how will she write a message?

Dolores finds herself thinking: I must teach myself to read and write. It cannot be so difficult. I taught the rudiments to Astra and Portia before the urge to return to the world of work and advancement recaptured my soul and I sent them off to professionals to finish my handiwork. It occurs to her that Gerald showed little inclination to introduce his first daughter to the wonderful universe of verbs and adjectives and nouns and subjunctive clauses that he supposedly inhabits as a citizen of that wordy world. Another failure to list in the annals of his shoddiness and treachery.

So now she must teach X. She must somehow force this tiny, illiterate, innumerate creature with her limited horizon to look at things in a new light that is comprehensible to her resident human, her live-in partner, her other half. She must learn to see things in a way that a captive mind or soul can interpret.

X must learn what two legs know to be good.

Portia is tapping something.

A message has arrived and if Dolores could read it she would scream, grab the tablet, call the police.

"I wait at Kentish Town tube station but you dint come, you naughty girl! I was looking for a girl just like you and me but you weren't there. It makes me a bit sad. Don't you trust me? I have had such a difficult time and I know that we could be such good friends. Aren't you sometimes lonely, too? But remember. This is our secret. I will wait every . . ."

Portia has tapped something but then makes the worm of incomprehensible gray-on-white jumble retreat on itself, devour its own tail. As X sometimes pretends to do during her spinning, performance-art show-offs, hurtling in tight, furry circles until she is breathless.

Portia switches off the tablet.

Voiceless, Dolores cries out: leave it on, leave it on! But Portia looks at her quizzically.

"It's not suppertime yet, X, you greedy cat. What are you yowling for?"

For long, dark hours I am able to avoid the large, male biped and I know that is the wisest course of action. But it will not be possible forever.

In her human configuration, Dolores Tremayne has reserves of rage that enable her to sustain anger and distance over long, icy periods of dispute. On the occasions when her man has overstepped some modest bound, she has succeeded in bringing him back into line with pursed lips and clipped responses that coax forth the ever-present latent guilt of the male who knows, deep down, that he has sinned in some way or another for that is the human condition.

X, by comparison, is a pussy. What else would she be?

"Treats, X," the novelist is purring. It is, she believes, the day after some incident that caused alarm. There has been the long slumber, the murmurs and squeaks of the night hours. X has prowled and patrolled the nocturnal home, stopping by her bowl to nibble at some pellets, check on her teenage and preteen charges, curling close to their sleeping forms to chase away the nightmares and the boogeymen.

Now, she detects the rattling of the cylindrical container associated with smells of sea and mollusk that her DNA deems to be irresistible.

Dolores is screaming: no, no, no.

But X is purring, indifferent to the trap.

The treats draw X closer.

One, a sampler, is from her husband's hand. The next is laid in her transportation cage.

X does not like the cage, because it has taken her to unpleasant encounters with bipeds in white jackets who cause pain and discomfort in return for money. But she likes the treat more. She snuffles and snoots, undone, like so many humans, by her nostrils.

The cage clicks shut behind her at exactly the moment she locates her fix of prawn and ocean.

"Walkies, X," Gerald Tremayne is saying in a voice that humans would call a snarl.

"Time to meet some wuff-wuffs."

eight

The world through the grille. Life chopped and quartered into squares. Sliced and diced. I am reminded of an ancient portcullis from the point of view of a besieged defender, looking out at a hostile horde readying towers and trebuchets, battering rams and ballistae. But how can X know that? Where did that idea, those soldierly words, come from?

X has been lured into the transportation box and me with her. We fit cozily, haunches to the rear, head facing forward, tail curled around like a huge traveling rug. I peer through the latticework of the door that has snapped shut on us, its catches firmly in place to forestall escape. I sense no panic from X. Not at first. She is used to this view, which usually precedes being placed on the big, pale seats of the car that covers distance without the expenditure of animal energy beyond the working of the controls—throttle, brake, brake, throttle; stop, usually at the place where the sado-biped prods and snips and probes with his sharp little devices and knuckled paws.

Makes me sick, in every sense.

Once, X had somehow contrived to devour the elasticated string used to hog-tie a rotisserie chicken as it turned on the spit. The cord had been cut and in the human rush to devour the hot, dead bird, the binding had fallen to the kitchen floor where X, smelling a delicious, rich, forbidden odor, proceeded to gobble it up, not even suspecting that its stretchy, nonorganic nature made it more or less indigestible.

"Where is the string?" Dolores asked in panic as X peered at her, licking her greasy chops.

"Oh, fuck. She's eaten the string!"

X was rushed in the Range Rover—by Dolores, not Gerald—to the rooms that smelled of alien quadrupeds, and injected with something that induced her to vomit. And up came the string! In human terms, it would be like swallowing a length of mountaineer's rope from the flanks of Mount Everest and then being forced to regurgitate it.

Bipeds rarely grasp the magnitude of such brushes with the unimaginable.

This time there is no Range Rover, no comforting hum of engine and automatic seven-speed gearbox, no gentle rhythm of tire on tarmac. X is bombarded with unfamiliar impressions from ear and eye and nostril. The world sways to Gerald Tremayne's gait as he leaves the apartment, walks along the narrow path leading to what I know to be eight hundred acres of North London heathland, but which X does not know at all.

Gerald walks with a degree of urgency, passing by all my memories which I can no longer articulate—the huge magnolia tree, heavy with blazing white blossoms in its brief season, the frail-looking bench in the little spinney where I have often retreated from family tensions to smoke a clandestine cigarette, the array of blooms, the towering semi-blighted ash trees that form the frontier between public land and our private communal gardens.

Azaleas, roses, shrubs tended by an army of noisy gardeners with leaf blowers and lawn mowers; sacks for fallen leaves and cropped grass; chain saws that howl with malice. Past the rhododendron, the fir tree, the *Escallonia*, the *Buddleia*, the *Ceratostigma*—names I know because I once served as secretary on the gardening committee of our residents' association, before my business success gnawed away at my availability for unpaid labor, banished any thought of "giving back" while there was still the prospect of taking salaries and bonuses and stock options in quasi-industrial proportions. And what else got consumed in this pell-mell rush for power and fame and riches? What other bonds and ties and nurtured interplays of texture and color became unraveled? Where else did my time disappear?

Don't go there, Dolores, not now; not while your children are being drawn into a webbed world and your husband seems to have expanded his sphere of influence among the neighbors.

Really. Do NOT go there because the possibilities are endless.

Who else? The maid from Manila? Your friends with their broken marriages and singleton yearnings for a head on the shared pillow and a hand to clasp the neglected buttock? Old school memory-laners? Ex-partners on exploratory missions? Chance encounters? Pub pickups?

Gerald swings the cage and we, X and I, are treated to a dizzying view of sky and cloud above other apartments in our complex. It is like being at a mid-twentieth-century funfair, the kind you see in old black-and-white films (though not if you are a cat) where people sit in swing boats and pull on ropes to send themselves to giddy heights, craving the thrill of life beyond the horizontal where only some frail semblance of G-force prevents them from tumbling earthward. He reaches the small, metal gate. A new vista: narrow bars perceptible through the caged doors, as if the cell is opening and the prisoner is filled with inchoate terror at what lies beyond.

Free Nelson Mandela! The crowds await, heaving and bursting and pushing and shoving in anticipation of the first glimpse. Free Dolores Tremayne!

Gerald punches in the numeric code. Inside my furry new persona, I cannot recall it. Numbers have slipped from my data banks, although the human me, on the road in Munich or Detroit or Shanghai, virtually lives in an arithmetical, algorithmic world of computations. Excel spreadsheets, profit, loss, projections; the universe reduced to the math of money. EBITDA, gross, net, amortization, letters that open computer programs, numbers that open gates, just as his patter once unlocked my heart.

The human me knows the answer to the riddle of the gate's opening but X, confronted with such routines, is mystified, defeated before the battle has even begun.

Gerald pushes through the gate, swinging the transportation box dangerously close to a clump of nettles.

Gate fever.

In truth, the status accorded to cats has always baffled Gerald. He does not get it. Cats are a waste of space. They do nothing, give nothing, give nothing away. They are creations of humans who project peculiar, attractive qualities onto the feline emptiness. Cats remind him of actors mouthing parts invented by others; superb performers; mirrors of our secret desires. Even the world's greatest brains—Einstein, for example—have been fascinated by cats. Or rather by the idea, posited by some Austrian physicist, that a single cat could at once be alive and dead, according to theories of quantum mechanics which, frankly, Gerald could live without. What was he called, the Austrian, who had somehow argued that if you put a cat in a steel box with a radioactive source and some poison, the cat would, by the theory of quantum superposition, be simultaneously subject to two contrary interpretations: alive or dead. For a moment he toyed with the idea, imagining X as the quantum cat, dispensing with the complexities, locked in a steel box with polonium-laced treats that would allow only one interpretation of her state of being: former, an ex-cat, a dead parrot.

Then there was that colleague of Dolores's who had been posted to a new job as a lobbyist in Brussels and had been obliged to embark on the rituals of household removals—the surly packers, the clumsy unpackers, the chipped porcelain, the hanging around for enormous tips. All of that had been covered, of course, by the firm. But the one riddle—not the quantum riddle—lay in working out how to transport the family cat, a superior type of cat, a Russian Blue called Marley. Of course Marley has all the requisite vaccinations and certificates of rabies-free health to cross just about any frontier. But the simplest, most elegant solution that Dolores's colleague could devise was to send him by cab. Not alone, of course. Marley would be escorted in the voluminous rear compartment of one of those new black cabs made by Mercedes, escorted across southern England, through the various controls for animals and humans at Folkestone, into the brief darkness of the Channel Tunnel and across the six-lane highways of northern Europe where gallant American GIs and British Tommys fought Fritz the German Hun with depressing regularity. Thus would Marley arrive in Brussels, peering from the smoked-glass windows at his new home city with much the same sense of ineffable superiority as a visiting president in a motorcade contemplating the unfamiliar sights of a minor ally or defeated foe.

But what was the Austrian called? Schirnding? Schopenhauer? Schiller? Schöneberg? Gerald halts for a quick séance with his cell phone's search engine.

Schrödinger!

Erwin Schrödinger! (1887–1961)

Unaware of her perilous superposition, neither one thing nor the other, yet both at the same time, X peers out of the cage with a combination of curiosity and abject terror. It is an environment she has yearned for instinctively without being able to know it objectively. Its surfaces are uneven, seething with smells of small life. Its upper limit is far higher, intangible. It is so much wider. It has no ceiling. There are none of the stages of the human cross—eating, sitting, sleeping, shitting, staring at moving pictures in a box. There is no box, in fact. If you were to be located out here, or left out here, you would not know which way to go. Which way to turn! You would have so many options. How would you navigate? What would you eat? Where are the bowls of pellets and the device that pumps potable liquid from a spout? Where are the soft surfaces for naps and the rough posts for scratching? The defecatory litter?

She observes other quadrupeds which attach bipeds to their necks with slender leashes and tug them along. They come in many shapes and sizes, some not much bigger than X herself, small legs pumping in a blur of fur. Others are huge, towering, slow-moving, Jurassic beasts, ambling along as if the world was theirs, with their lolling tongues hanging like slices of raw veal. A barrage of odors. All hostile. Even the small ones. Atavistically inimical to feline interests. A cacophony of noises. Names, apparently. "Hugo," "Algernon," "Fenton," "Milly." All called out with a variety of biped anxiety or wrath or entreaty. "Barney," "Bodger," "Bentley," "Bailey," "Charlie," "Buddy," "Bella," "Daisy," "Princess," "Rosie," "Gonzo," "Gizmo," "Sadie," "Seeley." There has been talk in the biped world of cats using similar leashes to exercise their patrons, to distract them from the instinctive feline pursuit of lizards and rodents and flying things. As if! Just think for a moment of all those noises in addition to the bellows and wheedlings of the dog world. "Tigger," "Tiddles," "Marie," "Berlioz," "Mephisto," "Eliot," "Munkustrap," "Quaxo," "Bombalurina."

"Pussy-cat," "Poo-cat," "Macavity," "X."

Canine Studies. Dogography 101. Despite the appearance of immense stupidity, these quadrupeds have nonetheless trained their bipeds to use flexible devices to lob spheroids over great distances without changing course. The quadrupeds retrieve these objects and reward the bipeds' skills in throwing them by returning them to feet encased in green rubber. With practice, the bipeds become increasingly skilled in the art of throwing, and go on to pursuits known as cricket and baseball, rarely thanking their canine trainers as they acknowledge the polite applause and the raucous roars of their supporters. With the frequency of this ritual, some of the spheroids have become layered in mud and saliva. They are not pleasant to behold. Even from afar, their odor is repulsive.

Sometimes the quadrupeds test the bipeds by withdrawing the favor of the returned spheroid, preferring instead to gallivant and gambol among themselves, tails wagging, snouts yapping, inducing panic in bipeds appealing desperately for the four-legs-good to reward them.

X notes that the quadrupeds have a curious means of communicating, prodding their noses into the rear ends of other quadrupeds. Disgusting! What do they say, hear? Information may be transmitted through the olfactory organs. Obviously enough. But surely these quadrupeds cannot derive pleasure from the odors of evacuation. Have they no sense of decorum? Or shame? Do they not acknowledge the essential privacy of bodily functions? They approach tall-growing things—larger versions of those she knows at home—cocking legs or squatting to urinate at will. No dark boxes here for the secret business of doing one's business. No scrambled litter and furtive ablutions. No self-respect.

They halt, willy-nilly, to deposit waste without regard for fellow creatures. And why should they worry when they have trained their bipeds to retrieve their droppings and carry them in little plastic bags like Bond Street shoppers bearing delicate and highly priced items?

X is surprised by the comparison she makes, since she has no idea what shops are or what they are for. Or where or what Bond Street is.

Now they are passing an expanse of water so huge that, for X, it might be the Pacific, but which is known to Dolores as a pond where dogs are allowed to leap in and retrieve sticks, then emerge to shake themselves as close as they can to their owners, or roll on their sides and backs in grass that may or may not be littered with canine feces that the biped collection process has overlooked. By accident or design.

X notes that one notable area of teaching in which the quadrupeds have singularly failed is in their attempt to introduce the bipeds to water. No matter how often the quadrupeds induce their patrons to lob the spheroids into the various tracts of pond life with their resident populations of duck, swan, teal and coot, the bipeds refuse to follow, preferring to loiter on the bank and be sprinkled by the quadrupeds as they shake themselves dry. The bipeds, it seems, are inherently terrestrial, and faintly masochistic, beings.

But it would be wrong to generalize. Out here, there are clearly subdivisions of the biped species. Some are clearly dangerous, not to be trusted alone, guarded by mobs of quadrupeds to keep them under control, tied to them by multiple leashes, like Gulliver tethered by Lilliputians, as if they are being restrained because of the hazard they present and their otherworldly strangeness.

Other bipeds are not contained at all. They do not even keep company with quadrupeds. They seem to represent a separate breed with legs of pale flesh that has no fur, just a freckling of hair that would never keep the cold at bay.

Dogography. Jogography. The biped fear of immobility, inertia—states of being prized by the higher species, such as cats.

By contrast to the essential stillness of much of X's day, these bipeds are in a state of constant agitation. Their legs scissor in an anguish of haste. Some are in such dread of the openness, the void, that they have taken to wheeled contraptions that carry them along, forcing their feet to revolve on mechanical treadmills. They pedal, swerve, curse, ring bells. Ting-a-ling.

Two legs bad.

Two wheels worse.

Through the feline audio system, Dolores hears snatches of conversation that make her cry for help, though all that emerges is a forlorn mew.

"So I am . . . like and . . . whatever."

Young girl voices recounting Facebook dramas they pursue on Twitter by way of WhatsApp and Instagram. A language unknown to Dolores growing up in the time of the Discman. Pre-mobile. Pre-touchscreen. Pre-selfie.

They pass them descending as Gerald ascends Kite Hill, hoping in his darkest thoughts that he will find Pit Bull Open Day underway at the summit, with legions of canine killers unchained.

Dolores feels like a message in a bottle that no one will ever open, destined to bob forever on shoreless oceans, a voice inside a cat crying for human help through a feline larynx.

"And Loretta and Alice were . . . like."

Sound bites of modern living, played out in the privacy of bedrooms, hunched over communications devices, swiping and tip-tapping in predictive text, uploading images, howling in protest when others are uploaded. Boasts. Sullen silences. Status changes. Meet me at Kentish Town tube station. I am a young girl just like you. Dolores feels an unease she cannot define. Even beyond the awful premonitions of Gerald's plan.

"And Toby was . . . kind of . . . naked?"

The rising interrogative tone of the postmodern sentence. Discuss.

Through her highly developed sonic facility, X detects sounds that vary from the remotely familiar to the totally incomprehensible. She has no means of defining the distinctions as those of language. She cannot know that, as they progress, they are mingling with people of far-flung origins in Minsk or Moscow or Metz or Munich or Manila or even Manchester. Humanspeak is universally indecipherable beyond its suggestions of mood. As they progress, the air fills with snatches of French and Italian and Polish and Croat and Mandarin. Wary Russians skirt expansive Spaniards along the tended pathways. Dolores wants to scream or howl or mew, but the bipeds are enclosed in their own recounted dramas.

Like Volodya told Miguel about Fifi that time in Shanghai?

So I said to the producer I needed my agent's sign-off on that.

Entre nous.

Just between the two of us.

And it turned out. Kind of.

Like chlamydia?

But you never told me.

Not that she ever cared. Mother. Or Father for that matter.

And go south in the winter. But where? Where is safe? These days.

Signboards to the meaning of life.

X senses a greater pace, or urgency. Gerald is stretching his loping stride to the cusp of a jog. The acceleration is alarming for cat and hidden passenger alike. What is he planning?

He is making sounds that a vestige of wifely consciousness recognizes as song.

Everybody wants to eat a cat.

Oh dear.

X sees other creatures she knows she should pursue and hunt, red in tooth and feather. Dolores lists them as she was taught one early, cold morning.

Dawn Chorus Day. The one day of the year when you venture forth in the crepuscular muzziness with the guide who knows all the names of all the winged creatures under the rising sun.

Oh, for the innocence of it. Wrens, tits, woodpeckers of various hues, coots, moorhen, ducks (plain and mandarin), nuthatch, breeding swans with mom on egg duty and pop on patrol, blackbird, magpie, crows, ravens, pigeons, doves, a kestrel, a swarm of invading parakeets. Black birds walking like robed priests. Who said that? Gulls that swoop and call, far from crashing surf or shingly beach or windblown marsh. Doves that mate in a nanosecond flurry. Twitchers—birders they prefer to be called—in their baggy cargo pants, stalking their prey with field glasses that magnify them out of all proportion. Is it only birds they seek to spy on in this land of young girls on secret walks and young boys rolling spliffs and drinking stolen cider?

Bring it all back, Dolores is thinking. Bring my life back.

Bring me back.

Gerald has drawn to a halt on Kite Hill. The place teems with bipeds of all sizes. Some are trying in vain to imitate the winged creatures, holding up scraps of bright material with tails and long strings that try to climb into the vast, blue dome above them, lofted by invisible forces. Are they hoping to fly? Will they be lifted off, high above London, like so many Mary Poppinses? Will they be eaten by enormous Brobdingnagian cats?

Wind in the east, foretelling times of change, upheaval.

Gerald places the transportation box on the ground where an unfamiliar element ruffles X's pelt, bombards her nostrils. He takes off his denim jacket and lays it on the ground next to the transportation box and stretches his long, lanky frame alongside it. Dolores feels X shrink back from the latticed door where an enormous wet black nose has just introduced itself with a growl and a bark like a clap of thunder.

"Nice doggie," Gerald says, ruffling the long hair around the neck of a German shepherd that bares its teeth by way of response.

Dolores recalls another wildlife list—Rottweilers, Dobermans, pit bulls, Staffies, Russells, Pointers. Lurchers. Weimaraners. Tiny Shih Tzus. Schnauzers with Falstaffian beards. Retrievers with soft mouths. Guard dogs with hair-trigger rage. Attack dogs boiling with bloodlust. All of them leash-free in the bright breezy world beyond the transportation box.

"Lots of nice wuff-wuffs, eh, X?

"Had to make a plan, X. After that stunt in the bedroom. One of you had to go. Tails, you lose. Cat-o'-nine-tails. And nine lives and now they ran out. I guess every dog has his day. Cats, too. An accident, I'll have to say. How you escaped, and then what? Flattened by the two-one-four bus? Disappeared? We can put up signs around the neighborhood—pictures of you with your big blue eyes. But no one will find you, of course, because you'll be the dog's breakfast by then. Ha-ha. And we'll get a new little pet. Maybe a budgerigar or something with no teeth. And they'll forget you in time."

The killer's lament. I didn't want to. He/she forced me to do it. It was for the best. Don't you see? The only way. A clean decisive moment. The final solution.

"What a pretty pussy."

A new human voice. Unfamiliar but not hostile. Female. Comforting.

"Indeed," Gerald is saying.

The woman—girl?—is squatting on her haunches next to the transportation box. Her voice has a faintly European lilt to it—Germanic, Nordic? She has blond hair and blue eyes and clear skin. She has been peering through the latticework, into the dungeon. X has been opening and closing her equally blue eyes to signal instant affection. Gerald shifts his lower body to suggest a similar reaction.

"Gerald," Gerald says, sitting up and offering his hand in friendship and preliminary maneuver.

OMG, Dolores is thinking. You are still stained from the upstairs bitch and now this!

The girl-woman extends her hand. Then pauses as her eyes widen to impossible dimensions.

"I know you," she blurts. "Gerald Tremayne. The novelist! *Birth* was sooo beautiful. You signed it for me at Hay. I listened to your talk. I can't believe it."

Dolores can vaguely remember. X, of course, has no idea what is going on. Bipeds are an odd bunch. Their moods shift inexplicably, and something is now intangibly different. The coordinates have switched, slipped, flipped. Unintended consequences govern events. How can X know that the intervention of this biped has saved her from release into the open where the quadrupeds would have hounded her and run her to ground and torn her to shreds, as surely as . . . as what?

As a foxhunt with dogs, Dolores tells her, as a terrier with a rat, a Russell with a rabbit, a leopard with a kudu. But X does not hear. What is a fox, terrier, Russell or leopard to a flat-cat? What is a hunt to a creature that lives from bowl to bowl, from pellet to pellet, delivered on schedule, multiple squares a day?

"Of course," Gerald is now saying. "You came up after the talk. You already had the book. To Sabina."

" 'With warm regards for the future,' " she recalls. "Omigod. You remembered my name!"

"From Austria. Linz. Of course."

The girl-woman almost swoons.

Dolores looks more closely through her cat's eyes. There are no dark roots in the apparition's fur; even her eyebrows are tantalizingly, naturally blond. How different can this be, in expectation, from Gerald's marital crossing of colors, their long bodies stretched side by side, chiaroscuro?

Is it because she is white? Or is it just because he is who—and what—he is? Pheromones. Testosterone. Unseen, undeniable comingling in the air between them, in their glances and subliminal messages. The urge to touch. Hold.

And she is young enough to be his daughter.

" 'And the future is now!' " The girl-woman giggles in wide-eyed wonderment. There is no malice, no aforethought. It has just happened. A miracle. Across a crowded hill, full of dogs and walkers.

"I can't believe it, Mr. Tremayne."

"Gerald. Please. Call me Gerald."

There is a pause. Beyond the grille of the transportation box, X is aware of the quadrupeds with their panting halitosis and hyper-lubricious tongues and enormous white teeth fixed in jaws that have evolved to seize the necks of bulls and not let go. What chance for a tiny fluffy cat among such creatures?

"Do you often do this? Gerald? When you are writing?"

Oh, if only I could answer that question for you, Mr. Tremayne! Gerald!

Dolores's memory is generating an inner slideshow of episodes that she now sees without the benefit of the doubt or of any doubt at all; moments at book fairs, in restaurants, on trains, airplanes, on street corners, book tours, family vacations goddammit, when apparently chance conversations led to absences for which she had blithely, trustingly sought no explanation and for which only the flimsiest explanations had been offered. Like that time in Devon when the girls were tiny and Gerald went off in search of ice cream and came back hours later with nothing to show for his foraging because the 99-er ice creams had melted and the chocolate wafers had all fallen into the sand. What a fool she had been!

"Well, you know," Gerald ventures, "I guess it just falls to me to make sure that this little creature has some quality of life . . . now that my wife is . . . away."

The word *away* plops into the sentence like a depth charge, heavy with enormous consequences. He has switched his facial expression from "aw, shucks—fancy little old me in charge of the family cat" to "flinty gaze into middle distance, denoting an irreducible core of pain that might only be salved by the touch of a virgin."

My wife is *away*, for which read mad, faithless, imprisoned for some awful ill-defined crime. Away with the fairies. With her best friend's husband. With the gurus of rehab, the high priests of therapy. Away with a yo-ho-ho and a bottle of gin. Away in the realms of Gabriel or Beelzebub depending on the final judgement. Anything but: away on a business trip to earn the money that pays the bills and keeps the coke dealer in custom.

When they met in the northeast of England, she had been doing a double honors course in Eng. Lit. and Business Administration, prior to her MBA in London. He worked on the maintenance staff, a roguish, raffish, piratical figure often compared by undergraduates to the actor Johnny Depp—long-haired, twinkly eyed, laden with knowledge of the kind they did not teach in their academic courses. Such as where the better quality of narcotics could be had, the safest E, the purest Charlie—("Smack I don't do," he would say haughtily. "Crack neither.")—transactions he liked to define as a legitimate redistribution of wealth from the bourgeoisie, in the form of its offspring, to the proletariat, represented by himself. Plus handling charges to offset the obvious risks.

A diamond in the rough, awaiting her tender attentions to cut and polish to human perfection.

She knew him from his association with Clarissa Fawcett, her college roommate—locally rooted and well-versed in the wiles of men of Gerald Tremayne's background—from whom he extracted a substantial chunk of the money sent by her parents for scholarly maintenance, arriving in his white van and dropping by their shared digs, his leather belt-pouch laden with narcotic offerings hidden among the camouflaging cargo of hammers, pliers, screwdrivers, spirit levels, wrenches.

Dolores did not approve of his secret trade. In her native Camden, where she had attended the prestigious girls' school, she had seen the results of his business at close quarters, among friends who battled in vain against the lure of skunk and E and K, uppers, downers, killers. She had seen the way the drugs warped minds, dictated behavior and scuppered moral standards as her friends fell victim to the promise of easy highs to banish teenage lows, craving transportation—trips, sometimes—to alternate worlds where doubt was banished and colors merged and people chilled. Whence there was no return.

When she realized why the dashing Gerald visited Clarissa, she was at first quite shocked that the handsome, soi-disant maintenance man was no more than the penultimate link in a chain of supply and demand that started on distant plantations of opium poppies, and coca plants and marijuana bushes, and led through hydroponic labs closer to home and tiny weighing scales in shuttered rooms to the end product sold to her friend in slender paper wraps and little plastic bank bags. Every step along the way contained the seeds and fruits of extreme violence, borne by the promise of easy money in fabled amounts. She felt angry that her friend's friend had duped her into assuming that he was simply a visitor, an admirer, a gentleman caller from a nonacademic but wholesome blue-collar, salt-of-the-earth universe of manual work and support for soccer teams and pubs and pints.

In part, Dolores's annoyance—at her roommate as

much as at Gerald—drew on her pity for hapless mules caught with condoms of cocaine bursting in their guts, and foolish British grannies who believe that the gift of a statuette from a Thai lothario was no more than that—certainly not an instant qualification for a near-certain death sentence. Back home, the streets around the market stalls at Camden Lock seemed so exotic and buzzy to foreign visitors who flocked there in great numbers to buy junk clothing and seek the frisson of proximity to danger, among the crowds of spindly dealers in baseball hats and bulky law enforcement officers in Kevlar vests designed to thwart knife attacks. But to Dolores, these same thoroughfares and dark corners were a totem of failure—the failure of her people to rise above the trap of being poor and bereft of prospects, gallery exhibits for visitors from Europe who, their hungers sated, would return to better worlds where societies looked after their own and did not abandon them to wasted lives.

She loathed the sight of young people (often black—in fact, usually black) being patted down by the police in the back streets near Camden tube station on the Northern Line. The skeletal women with track-marked arms and ferret eyes, panhandling among the tourists, filled her with rage at the suppliers. At people, in fact, just like Gerald Tremayne.

And yet Gerald had a way of explaining it away. It was a sideline. He would not sell to people who could not afford. He did not do the really hard stuff. Recreational was all. Among people whose college years would inevitably end in degrees and good jobs and a return to sanity in homes where the favored drug was Chablis or Chardonnay or, at worst, gin and tonic. Of course, he felt guilt-stricken about it, but, in these blighted parts where the shipyards were shuttered and the mines were sealed, what choice was there? If you went to the job center and told them you wanted another chance—a sixth-form college, maybe, a proper apprenticeship in a real trade—they would laugh at you. So, yes, briefly and not forever, he did this hateful, hated business. His dealing was no more than the equivalent of Steve McQueen's baseball in *The Great Escape*, pounding the prison walls. He was saving his earnings to get out. To concentrate on his real love—writing! He was building a stash of cash for his flight south to London and beyond—Paris and the grave of Jim Morrison; Tangier and Marrakech and Fez; the trail east through Istanbul to the ashrams of India. Okay, he had no fancy qualifications. But when he sat in the back of his white van, parked up in a lay-by, scribbling down his thoughts and ideas in pilfered notebooks, he knew for sure that his words made sense, wove spells, signposted the future. At home, in the bedroom he shared with a younger brother, he kept a laptop locked away under the bed and, late at night, began to transfer his notes into the outline, the framework of a plot, a story, a narrative. The baleful light from the screen lit up a face filled with amazement that he, Gerald Tremayne, no-goodnik, drug pusher, could build these fantastic phantoms that strutted the stage of his invention. The first seeds of *Birth* had been planted.

When he told her this—his deepest secret—his eyes lit up with missionary zeal that sent a thrill through her. He was a storyteller whose story was his own. A pied piper.

More than anything, he told her, he wanted out of this postindustrial penitentiary where he unblocked vomit-clogged student lavatories, replaced lightbulbs in dormitory corridors, fixed doors smashed and splintered in savage drunken paroxysms. Dolores took him at his word, believing that she was the only person with whom he shared this inner life of yearning and creativity. Because he told her so. Because he was a man of many personae to be buffed and polished and presented as needs dictated.

His needs, of course.

In his role as campus handyman, Gerald had access and cover for his covert trade and his skilled seduction. There were many lewd jokes about him. Envious male undergraduates spoke of his rattling the pipes, plumbing the depths, oiling the hinges. But, to Dolores, he offered a different face. When he discovered from her roommate that she was studying literature, he began to pepper his conversation with references to poets and writers, Dylan Thomas and D. H. Lawrence—provincial men who had made good through language and their mastery of it. Finally, one day, he had brought her a USB stick. Read it, please, he wheedled in his Geordie accent. Tell me where I am going wrong. At first she resisted. She was not dumb. She knew his reputation from her roommate who told her explicitly to be careful where Gerald was concerned. And anyhow, she was a student, not a teacher. What would she know about first novels and literary pretensions? Maybe he saw the USB stick as the key to other things. There were few people of color on campus. Maybe he wanted a trophy. Well, look, I'll just leave it here, he said, placing the USB on her desk one day when he dropped by to sell her friend a baggie of the best hash in New-castle. Up to you. Take it or leave it. Read it, if you like. Or not.

So she did, and it was not half bad, Dolores thought, surprised at the quality of the writing from the roughneck Tremayne, despite her desire to harbor no intellectual prejudice against the handyman-genius who had pirou-etted into her life on paint-spattered, steel-capped boots, sneaking up on her while she was wrestling with economic theory and Milton. And sold class-A drugs to her fellow students, recruiting some of them as runners and decoys.

Gerald became something of a fixture, offering dis-counted dope to Clarissa, sipping many cups of tea and coffee with Dolores, knowing, in the way that lotharios know and believe to be their right and destiny, that he did not need to hurry, that she would fall into his arms in the fullness of time if he took things easy, but would run a mile if he came on too strong. And she knew, too, that sooner or later, but preferably later, after a decent inter-val of circling and due diligence, they would tumble to-gether when trust had built a carapace against the fear of exploitation or rejection. Against betrayal. The most hei-nous of outcomes.

"It won't last," Clarissa said with the finality of un-assailable conviction, beyond challenge or debate. "I know the type. Love you and leave you. You're probably only thinking about it to annoy your dad. Or something Freudian or whatever."

While her roommate busied herself with rolling mari-juana into a perfect reefer, Dolores considered her taunt-ing proposition. What did she know about Freud? Or whatever? Clarissa was studying criminology, even as she committed crime to distract herself from the rigors of her course. She had her eye on a career in the police. Know thine enemy! But, Dolores conceded with some reluctance, Clarissa might have a point.

As an adolescent Dolores had seemed to bypass the rebellious phase. A model daughter. Good grades. No unexplained all-nighters. No motorbike howl to signal the arrival of an unsuitable suitor in greasy leathers athwart some overpowered machine. So maybe, belatedly, this was her gesture, her catch-up revolt against parental—paternal—authority. Against all her father's hints of African dreams and re-nurtured roots in a faraway never-never land.

Roots! Her roots were in Camden or Newcastle, not Johannesburg or Cape Town. So why not make that clear with her rough-edged, flat-voweled beau.

"Not really," she said. "Not really Freud."

They were sitting in their shared sitting room, cluttered with Dolores's books and her roommates' bongs and the familiar accoutrements of student life: folders and files stacked neatly in Dolores's sphere of influence; empty takeout boxes on Clarissa's.

"Well what then?" Clarissa inquired, firing up her creation and inhaling deeply.

It was a good question.

Maybe it was just her genes demanding non-conformism, rebellion. When her mother met her father, after all, he was not just some rebellious youth. He was a terrorist, a freedom fighter, the product of another continent, another race. Soviet-trained. Moscow rules! She was an English rose, her blue eyes passed down to her daughter in the mingling of chromosomes that sealed the parental bonding. He had grown up shoeless in Zululand; she had worn heels that tip-tapped on the cobblestones. He offered his hand. She defied her elders and took it, back in those days when such trysts were a novelty tantamount to revolt. So it was only natural that the child of this union would seek romance in a different milieu.

And she had found it—it had crept up on her, ambushed her—in this sharp-edged outcast with dreams far beyond the frontiers of his social legacy. If her father had yearned and struggled for political liberation through the barrel of a gun, then Gerald was the creative equivalent, struggling for the liberation of the words and phrases and sentences and paragraphs that poured forth with all the insistence and clamor of a Kalashnikov on automatic fire. And she, Dolores, would be his muse, his commissar, honing and channeling the inchoate passions. His Beatrice. She would not be the first upwardly mobile woman to fall for a man from lower on society's imposed ladder, seeking to escape a different world that doomed its inhabitants to narrow horizons and institutional mediocrity. If anything her father should be proud of her. Her love was a mighty blow for the class struggle, the fight for a society free of prejudice and injustice, the battle to dismantle the barriers of heritage.

"*Pygmalion!*" Clarissa suddenly barked from within her narcotic fug in one of those lightbulb-illuminating, penny-dropping, gotcha moments. "That's what it is, isn't it? Except it's in reverse. You're Henry Higgins and he's Mary Doolittle."

"Eliza. It's Eliza Doolittle. And. No. It's not *Pygmalion*."

But the notion settled, and with it the uneasy question of whether her heart's desire had become entangled with some strange evangelism. How many women, after all, devoted far too much of their energy and forgiveness to the enhancement and improvement of their chosen partner?

In the end, when she completed her studies, he offered to help her move her boxes and books and files and folders down to London. Gallantly, he declined her offer to pay for the diesel, resisting the counter-suggestion to go Dutch. As they left the northeast in his white van with its freckles of rust and belches of diesel fumes, she did not pay too much attention to his bulky tote bag and laptop computer that had somehow been packed along with her worldly possessions. Not to mention his battered toolbox with its shelves and nooks and crannies laden with all manner of equipment and widgets and pouches and baggies. The portable electric drill and its charger should have offered her a clue to his intentions, and perhaps it did, along with the thrill of knowing what could not yet be said out loud.

Companionably, happily, they bowled down the M1 and into North London. And there they stayed. To this day.

Surely, she told herself now, swaying and bouncing in the transportation box, it had not been all cynical on his part. Surely there had been love? Surely the arrival of the girls had placed their bonds and vows on a different, unassailable plane, built a palisade against temptation and all-too-easy conquest?

But when had it ended? How had she not seen his

roving-eye, his default setting, reasserting itself as she clambered the corporate ladder, rising into a stratosphere that offered no space for husband or family? Had he even waited the mandatory seven years before scratching the itch? At the beginning he had made his contribution. North London offered rich pickings for a man of his accomplishments—in many ways, she now suspected—and he soon had a client list of handiwork-challenged householders who reached for his cell phone number to deal with fused electrics and frozen boilers, broken sash windows and dripping taps, showers that backed up behind grease-trap drains. And then there was the second list of customers seeking edgy exhilaration or numbed torpor, often at the same addresses, just at different times of the day. Or night. Between those sorties, she heard him tap-tapping away with single fingers on the laptop, *Birth* building in range and might to its magisterial, soon-to-be-bestselling 630 pages of chronicles from the north, an early Knausgaard of detailed observation and generational dysfunction.

As he struggled with recalcitrant sentences and words that sent him rummaging through the thesaurus, he acquired an agent who stirred a flurry of interest at the Frankfurt Book Fair. The monkey wrench gave way to the workstation, the drill to the desk. Windows XP displaced window sashes, the rough diamond polished and faceted, the toolbox banished to the storeroom in the cellars below their mansion block. The client list for his potions narrowed to personal use, sustained by his allowance from the joint account she set up as success took her into the rarefied financial reaches where dependents became tax breaks. When a ballcock broke, or a water filter needed replacing below the white Belfast sink, he called in a plumber and watched with a mildly critical air as some artisan from eastern Europe completed a task he could just as easily have performed himself and to far better effect. Had he bothered to help when they had the kitchen renovated; or the big living room repainted; or when the shower rooms were rebuilt and replumbed; or when the bookcases were extended to make space for the foreign translations and manifold editions of *Birth*; or when the units around the fireplace were revamped to accommodate the wide-screen television which she often found tuned to the sports channels when he told her he had been hard at work on *Marriage*, or mapping out *Death*? And when had he last told her he loved her? And when, for that matter, had she uttered that same incantation, the three-word antidote to the entropy of passion?

They are nearing the end of the walk back from the jaws of death.

"And do you work from home, er, Gerald?"

"I have a little place. An office just across the road."

News to me, X heard an alien voice murmuring from somewhere inside her own head.

"I could show you if you like," he was saying. "I'll just drop off the cat."

Dolores feels the powerful bound of his long legs as he leaps up the stairs to their apartment, three at a time. She wishes Jenny Steinem, their neighbor, could see him now and share this knowledge of deceit. The door with its double Chubb locks swings open. The transportation box hits the floor with a thud on the sea-grass carpet. The portcullis door swings open and X stretches her way out of it, her bottom raised, her front paws spread before her, digging into the familiar roughness of the carpeting where her claws find easy purchase.

X turns back and does not grasp what Dolores sees through those bright, blue, rag-doll eyes. Gerald is removing the tape from the cat flap, the outer wall of the keep, the last bastion, the path to freedom and foxes and dogs and BMWs and the 214 bus pounding up and down the hill. Again, he has reached for the eat-me pellets of prawn, tuna, salmon, rabbit essences, laying a trail that leads to the flap.

"There you go, X. Enjoy," he says, swinging the flap open and closed with his sneakered foot. "I know I will."

In anyone else, she might admire the libidinous stamina, if not the bottomless capacity to deceive. If she had maintained her status as the object of the former, there would be no need for the latter. But, through her cat's eyes, the world has been turned on its head.

nine

Had he wanted it this way? Had it ever, really, not been this way?

Gerald Tremayne looked down into the cat's blue eyes and, for a second, thought he saw some distant yet familiar glimmer that disappeared as quickly as it flared. Reproach? Anger? Hurt?

Anthropomorphistic crap!

It was a cat. A cat that had, through its own doing, gotten in the way, interposed itself in matters that could only be resolved by its abrupt—yet explicable—demise. A kitten could, if necessary, be found to replace the soggy mass of redness and bloodied fur that would presently adorn the wheels of some fund manager's Bentley (nothing but the best for X, of course. As it had always been). Or even a puppy—sweet little demander of thrice-daily walks and opportunities for conversation with lonely dog owners only waiting to shed their Wellington boots and matching Barbour coats in clandestine couplings.

Of course, he would have to replace the cleaning lady,

too, since she, it would transpire, in her zeal unlocked the cat flap. He would personally interview potential successors, sketch out their responsibilities, his expectations of them. Or was that going a bit too far, sailing a bit too close to the wind?

This, he thought with a sudden, short-lived injection of melancholy and self-pity, was what his life had become. No wonder that the second volume of the trilogy was little more than an empty USB stick, a Word folder whose edit-trace described a dwindling parabola of deletions and deductions and excisions and subtractions and contractions that created a void, a zero, a chapter heading leading nowhere.

All work and no play.

Red Rum, Dead Cat.

It was a dark and stormy night.

How could anyone expect his genius to blossom between the cat litter and the school run? He had tried. God knows he had tried. But how often was irresistible temptation strewn across his path? Through no fault of his own. And now again. His burden. His gift to the world.

She was waiting outside the apartment house.

Ingrid? Eva? Brunhilde? Agata? Ulrika? Annette? Sabrina? Sabena?

Sabina.

She smiled prettily, slightly nervously.

"Sorry that took a moment. Had to settle the pussy down. There's always so much to do when you are, you know, alone?"

"Oh, I know," Sabina said. "You poor man."

Cast the line. Set the hook.

Glancing over his shoulder as they crossed the busy road that ran past the front garden of the apartment house, he caught a glimpse from the window above his own apartment of Jenny Steinem staring down at them. Shit. How to describe her expression? Puzzled? Aggrieved? Below her, in the bay window of his own living room, X had taken up position on a bookcase and was pawing at the window the way cats do, though there was something frenetic in her manner, something desperate. He waved casually.

"Who was that?"

"No one special. Just the cat," said the spider to the fly.

Sabina looked back.

"*Wie süß!*" she said.

"What?"

"How sweet. The way she paws at the window. As if she's saying, you know, good-bye. Like a lover." She giggled.

"Oh yes, a real sweetie. All I've got left in some ways."

She took his hand and squeezed it. Despite the recent adventure—perhaps because his neighbor had seen him cross the road with his putative conquest—he felt a responsive stirring, an ancient longing. Inextinguishable ardor. Unstoppable urge. Infinite erectility. He still had it. To share around. And the sooner Ms. Steinem got used to the idea, the better.

His writer's studio was his secret. So was the origin of his occupation of it—so duplicitous it sometimes made him wince at the audacity, or utter foolishness, of the arrangement, literally on his own doorstep, in his own backyard. Where you shit only to court extreme sanction.

It was the opposite, the direct contradiction of the Don Juan code: never linger or overstay your welcome; never betray your coordinates. No forwarding address, cell phone number. No means of subsequent contact for the delivery of recriminations or lawyers' letters. No accumulation of baggage that might hinder freedom of movement, frustrate the fleet of foot in quest of prey. Victims.

But that is where Mathilde de Villeneuve, the wealthy, wayward, onetime wife of a French diplomat, had brought him. The supreme danger. The ultimate challenge. The odd thing, he sometimes thought, was that apart from his wife, Mme. de Villeneuve was the closest thing he had ever had to a steady date, a relationship, a part of life that survived all the thrills and spills as a factor that must always be taken into account. Loath though he was to admit it, lothario had met his match.

It started like this.

Birth had been published to enthusiastic reviews but had not yet yielded a revenue stream, or advance payments on future creations, to completely replace the twin trades Gerald Tremayne had imported from the northeast: drug dealing and plumbing. In his workman's attire, belt on hip, toolbox in hand, he had been making a delivery of certain substances in his old white van to a well-heeled customer in Holland Park. He had been returning to his vehicle when he became aware of a voice calling out.

"Monsieur, monsieur."

He turned to confront the source of this alien tongue and was taken aback by the vison of Mathilde de Villeneuve in close-fitting workout clothes, fresh from what he later discovered to be a private gym in the basement of her mansion. Although she had called out to him in French, her English was fluent enough to explain to him, in some distress, that a blockage in the drains of her restaurant-sized kitchen was causing overflows of water just as members of her staff were preparing for an important banquet.

Could he help? Of course, he could help.

He followed her into the villa, marveling at its opulence— the black-and-white-checkered marbling of the entrance hall, the vast gleaming chandelier below the curved staircases leading to upper floors, the glimpses of huge salons with antique furnishings and tall windows that looked out over rose gardens.

So it really happens, he thought to himself. Like in the triple-X movies. *Beauty and the Beast.* The princess and the priapic plumber.

At the time of their initial encounter, he was, it is true, getting ahead of himself. Everywhere he turned as he went about the business of identifying and clearing the blockage, there seemed to be retainers and gardeners, chefs and sous-chefs, maids and secretaries. But, unlike others of her kind, she did not abandon him to some underling as he went about his work. She chatted. She questioned. Where did he live? Was this his only line of work? She had seen his van at her neighbor's home a few times and wondered what the problem was with next door's pipes and faucets. Or was it a delivery of a different kind? Something that she, too, might find interesting? He found himself talking about his writing and hinting at other, illicit confection he might supply. When, finally, he lay on his back under the offending sink, his lower body protruding onto the kitchen floor and his legs akimbo, he hoped she would at least speculate on what other attributes he might display in that same position in a more intimate setting. When she asked for his bill, he said not to worry. She asked where she could reach him again in the event of blockages that needed clearing. It was one of those turning points when you know you should cut and run but you don't. You know you should get out while the going is good and do the sensible thing. But he didn't. Instead, he gave her one of the visiting cards he had printed out from the internet—a rash departure from tradecraft. In that precise moment, he knew he was taking a gamble he would live to regret.

And there was another thing. No matter how posh she looked and talked and carried herself, he knew that, deep down, she was no more highborn than he was.

It took one to know one.

At the time, she was married to His Excellency the Ambassador of France to the Court of St. James, just as the indolence and misbehavior that marked his tenure were coming to the attention of both the Quai d'Orsay and various British law enforcement agencies. He had been awarded his diplomatic post as a reward for campaign contributions to a right-wing politician who ended up in the Élysée Palace as president. Gaston de Villeneuve had been of two minds about the job but his relatively new wife—his third—had persuaded him of the advantages, the glamour, the business contacts and the wonderful lifestyle that would accrue to them with the relatively

light lifting of canapés and the trade in banter and secrets. What he did not realize was that, even with his deep
pockets from a lifetime in the aeronautics industry, he
could not really afford the outgoings that the beautiful
Mathilde seemed to regard as her due. Even Gaston de
Villeneuve's substantial coffers would require some in-
formal replenishment.

When officials from Paris began to nose around a little,
they discovered that his appointments diary was little
more than a tabula rasa, while his official expense claims
resembled a gazetteer to the better shirtmakers of Jermyn
Street, the tailors of Savile Row and the bootmakers and
hatters of St. James's. Clearly, the ambassador extraordi-
nary and plenipotentiary was augmenting his salary and
his savings from some other source. But what could it be?

Mathilde de Villeneuve knew nothing of all this until
it was much too late. And so she played her role with conviction and artistry, the talk of the ambassadorial tread-
mill and of the writers of gossip and diary pieces in the
newspapers that took an interest in the lifestyle of the upper crust.

No one could quite pinpoint where she had learned her
diplomatic skills—certainly not in the seamy-steamy
quartier of Marseille where she had grown up. But she
performed the duties of a hostess with immense aplomb,
meeting, greeting, presiding over *placements* and menus,
wine choices and the ineffable sense of social manipulation
that shepherded guests from entrance to exit as the or-
molu clock on the ornate fireplace of her salon chimed
eleven and the carriages arrived to ferry the great and the
good away, flattered by her and envious of her husband.

Politicians and arms dealers, ambassadors and cultural icons from the worlds of opera and authorship, historians and editors processed through her soirees from the reception line to the fawning farewells. Like in those TV ads for gold-wrapped spherical chocolates served on silver platters. There was something icily formal in her official manner, regal, untouchable. She knew everyone but no one really knew her. Balanced between ostentation and perfect taste, they became known as one the most gilded couples on the diplomatic circuit.

Conversationally they were just as fluent with American billionaires discussing the latest season at the Hamptons as they were talking the inside politics of Damascus or Moscow or Tehran. They were regulars at Covent Garden for the opera and the ballet. They rarely missed Bayreuth or the new season at the Garnier. Their apartment back home in the 16th arrondissement of Paris was rumored to have been acquired by her forebears from the pashas of Egypt in some complex wrangling over the Suez Canal. (A version that did not quite coincide with this account spoke of a need among some of her father's business associates to cleanse cash flow through the real estate market in which, before her marriage to Gaston de Villeneuve, she had established a niche as a broker of bespoke residential properties.)

But when Gerald Tremayne crossed her threshold, he discovered another person altogether, a predator whose stalking outstripped his own by far, whose true identity swung between remarkable poles, never to settle or be truly defined. She floated like a butterfly, buzzed like a bee; flattered, cajoled, demanded, submitted. She entwined her conquests in the same obsessive needs as his class-A products. There were many Mathilde de Ville-neuves. None of them, he sometimes thought, was real. But if there was a single moment when he had sensed that his tragic error had been committed, it was on a strange and distant night in Kentish Town, in a place where un-known bands held their gigs in a room above a café. His Rubicon loomed before him and he jumped in with both booted feet.

Gerald Tremayne had been asked to give a reading of pages from *Birth,* streamed live over the internet. Dolo-res had been absent at a company off-site somewhere in Hertfordshire. The babysitter had been called upon to at-tend the girls, accepting the TV remote control as her badge of office along with instructions on lights out and a promise that his evening activities would not run late. If fortune favored him, he might bump into some groupie or literary hanger-on only too pleased to oblige. But Mme. de Villeneuve was not at the forefront of his consider-ations. Here, in Kentish Town, he was remote from her tribal hunting grounds.

His appearance was sandwiched between two bands— one a family concern of father and sons, with brother on drums, singing idealistic Afro songs from safer times; the other a raucous remix group made up of women in pink wigs. While the musicians busied themselves switching one set of instruments for another, and people recharged bottles of beer and plates of hummus and pita bread, Ger-ald perched on a high stool under a single spot, clutching his personal, much-annotated copy of *Birth,* with Post-it stickers marking the pages he liked to think of as his best.

He had dressed for the moment and the part—anguished author in tight, worn Levi's, corduroy jacket and black roll-neck—and knew that he cut a fine figure.

At first, in the darkened pool of faces staring at him from beyond the spotlight's penumbra, he had not recognized the woman with her ash-blond hair piled high in a confection of scarves and beads, strutting and preening on high platform shoes, perching on a high stool at the bar, pouting. When she slid a short black Gucci leather jacket festooned with chains off her shoulders, he became aware of a revealing V-neck T-shirt garlanded with an iron crucifix that dangled above her cleavage. When she turned to order a beer—bottle, no glass, she stipulated—he saw that the rear of the T-shirt, decorated with a sequined representation of a parrot, bore a motto in the manner of Hells Angels' biker gear: Dirty Deeds Done Dirt Cheap.

He heard someone mutter: "See the pole dancer's arrived."

And then realized who she was.

Everything about her presence bellowed danger, with hazard lights flashing. But he was a moth to her gaudy flame. As soon as his reading was done—with thankfully few questions about where his best ideas came from, and whether he wrote by hand or on a computer, and how long it took to write a book—he was at her side. They danced briefly to the music of the bewigged women's band. They left by hastily arranged signals to regroup at the Range Rover parked outside. They relocated to a dark corner near the graves of Highgate Cemetery. The babysitter earned generous overtime in return for a pledge of omertà.

Only later did Gerald Tremayne realize that he had never once mentioned to Mathilde de Villeneuve that he would be at the gig in Kentish Town that night. Somehow she had known where he would be, run him to ground in his North London lair. Ambushed, captured and caged him. Jekyll in Holland Park. And Hyde in Kentish Town. Or was it the other way around?

"Who was that woman at the reading? The one on the internet? The tarty one," Dolores asked when she returned from the off-site, having followed the wizardry of internet live streaming of the event from her hotel room at the company off-site.

"Beats me," he said.

"Wasn't that you dancing with her?"

"Dancing? I don't think so."

He took the Range Rover for a steam-clean of the rear seat and luggage bay. He sought to reestablish the protocols of separate lives. But the madness did not just stop there. How could it? Mathilde de Villeneuve would not allow it. He was not in control. She had offered to pay the lease on a place for their trysts, where he could work during her long absences, trotting the globe with her husband, from New York to Martinique to Saint-Tropez.

She could, of course, have chosen to rent a pied-à-terre—a foot on the ground, a bum on a bed—anywhere. Maybe somewhere closer to her residence in Holland Park. But she wanted somewhere discreet, remote, in some scruffier neighborhood where she ran no risk of running into anyone whose name figured in her Rolodex of the glitzy and the powerful. She wanted, perhaps, to slum it a little. She signed the lease under a phony name, in a building that offered rooms to lawyers and therapists. A gift for services rendered. And in return, she had first dibs. On him.

In the plotting of duplicity and the logistics of deceit, there were no lapses. No alibi went unrehearsed or untested; no telltale quirks of personal hygiene betrayed their couplings. But, in a manner neither of them could have foreseen, their liaison became collateral damage in the much more cataclysmic unravelling of her diplomatic idyll in Holland Park. The sins that brought down the complex construct of her double life were, paradoxically, her husband's, not her own. Her own transgressions left no trace.

French investigators inquiring into her husband's mysterious sources of unearned wealth discovered that their inquiries crossed paths with parallel sleuthing by private detectives scrutinizing his activities at an array of Mayfair gambling dens, where his winning streaks at the baccarat and blackjack tables had drawn the attention of the pit bosses and proprietors. In the aftermath, several croupiers were sacked and the diplomat's accreditation was withdrawn. He disappeared and retreated to regroup in the Cayman Islands. She made no attempt to follow him or track him down, leaving that mission to her lawyers.

There had been a brief flurry of tabloid interest that Gerald Tremayne found disconcerting, in part because it showed his lover's potential for uncompromising reactions to misfortune, for taking matters to extremes. When her husband was exposed as a wastrel, a cardsharp and God knew what else, the papers reported, she had spilled acid on the official ambassadorial Citroën and taken a razor to the Tricolore at the entrance to the residence. She had burst into the 11 a.m. meeting—morning prayers—at the embassy and accused her husband of committing acts of infidelity with a junior cultural attaché. Her behavior amazed those who knew her only as the diplomatic hostess. But the few who were privy to her upbringing— and recalled the fiery temper displayed by her mother in some of the more notorious establishments in Marseille— were not surprised at all.

As her public life went up in flames, Mathilde de Ville-neuve cashed in her prenup and withdrew to a private bolt-hole on Fifth Avenue in New York, where she had many friends who would offer sympathy for her misfor-tune and, perhaps, assist in the quest for a successor spouse. Left to his own devices, Gerald Tremayne tended the shrine of their passions in the apartment she had leased near his home in more intimate times, believing that, as he put it, the game was a bogey and he would know soon enough when the lease on his love nest was canceled. Until that time came, though, why not draw some benefit and solace from the whole sorry imbroglio?

The studio was large and airy, located on the fifth and top floor and reached by a small, caged elevator. My art-ist's garret, he liked to say, self-deprecatingly, as he es-corted guests through the entrance vestibule and in to a spacious loft, with en suite facilities and galley kitchen that commanded a view through half-closed venetian blinds over trees and gardens to the acres of heathland where he would soon be training the new puppy to retrieve sticks, balls and attractive, female fellow dog walkers. Perhaps, in homage to the memory of X they would call it Y, and only he would know the answer to the question: Y did X cross the road?

The desk was a solid board of white oak, mounted on trestles, with a large, silent computer monitor at center stage. As a reminder, he liked to say, of his roots, he had hung his old work belt with its pliers and screwdrivers on a wall, as if it were an artwork in its own right, an installation. Or perhaps a warning of the livelihood he would have to re-embrace if things ever got unmanageable. (There had been times when, like some medieval patron exercising droit de madame, his benefactor liked him to wear it, and little else—a throwback to the days when they met.) A coffee table was stacked with recent novels by other writers, grouped in homage around a final typescript of *Birth* from the publisher, bound in old-fashioned, predigital string. In a corner, a flat-screen television was positioned opposite a capacious sofa that doubled as a daybed toward which he steered her. A central switch controlled lamps positioned around the studio. He sat at his swivel chair and swung toward her, legs akimbo.

"So what do you think?"

"It is wonderful. To think that here such great work is done. Such bursts of words. Such flows of inspiration. Such literature. Oh my God," she said, picking up the typescript. "Is this really . . . ?"

He crossed the room to sit beside her, cozily, his muscular, tanned hands unknotting the simple binding on the typescript in her lap so that she could leaf through his work, his soul.

"I wouldn't normally show this. I'd forgotten it was here, in fact, but the way you spoke, your words, made me think: yes, she gets it! She understands! And that is so, so rare."

She leaned against him. The typescript slipped to the floor, its string unbound, its pages loose, but they were too focused elsewhere to discuss the finer points of its narrative structure, use of character, or composition.

ten

It is a test of wills that Dolores sometimes thinks she is winning and sometimes despairs of ever advancing. X, she has come to learn, is in thrall to appetites she can barely understand. From Gerald's perspective, that is her Achilles' heel. And now he has laid a trap to prove himself right.

A trail of treats leads to the newly liberated cat flap. X is following it with greedy enthusiasm, snuffling and munching her way inexorably toward the great barrier that separates her designated environment from the mysteries beyond it—her wardrobe to Narnia; her highway to the danger zone.

The trail ends in what Dolores knows to be a prawn and rabbit cocktail treat carefully balanced on the lower frame of the flap. X prods at the delicacy with an inquiring jab of a paw and, lo, the flap swings forth and back. The treat falls to the carpeted floor, where X devours it. It produces a sense of deep satisfaction—reminiscent, as far as Dolores can understand, of the first sip of a good martini

in the City Club in Manhattan, which she sometimes visits as a guest of business associates. Then it is gone. X
wishes to repeat the experience, to rekindle the sensu-
ous intimations of sea and burrow. She prods the flap
again. And again. It swings forth and back on an expanding parabola with every punch. The treat, perhaps,
lies beyond it. It is, perhaps, one of those moments she
associates with bipeds who offer gratification in return
for some learned procedure or action. Like defecating in
a box. Or scratching at a post. Or not urinating in the
base of a ficus tree. Responses structured for human con-
venience, according to principles enunciated initially, of
course, for the dogs whose salivatory habits helped the
Russian physiologist Pavlov define the conditioned reflex.
Such nuggets of general knowledge, Dolores finds herself
thinking in her lonely prison, are of little use in deterring
X from pursuing the association of flap and food. Already,
in other words, her reflex is conditioned. She will not need
a bell or a buzzer to make the link. She is, after all, much
smarter than any canine. But she is not so smart at all
because her responses are based on the absence of threat,
which is not how the real world functions. She is, in other
words, a stranger to calamity, while the world beyond her
immediate comfort zone overflows with jeopardy.

X punches the flap again and pushes her head through
the gap. She is now, more or less, committed to a course
of action that may or may not lead to a treat. Maybe not
the one she was programmed to expect, though. She is
halfway through the great barrier, her head protruding
into the area where the series of ascending and descending

horizontal planes enables bipeds to achieve upward or downward mobility. Her front legs rest on the lower frame of the flap.

No no no, Dolores is trying to scream, though sound is beyond her capabilities in this ethereal state of being. For a moment she thinks that X must resemble some gnarled farmer of preindustrial times, leaning companionably on a stable half-door to smoke a pipe, shoot the breeze, take the air, converse with passersby. Then she feels the muscles bunching in X's rear legs. There is a mighty shove, and sudden propulsion, like a stopper pushed out of a bottle by a buildup of bubbles.

Dolores struggles for the simile. She knows this. She knows precisely which liquid behaves in this manner. But at first she cannot recall it and she worries that the process by which she is seeking to humanize X is working in reverse and she is becoming felinized, losing her grasp on vocabulary, claimed by some mysterious, trans-species affliction—Katzheimer's.

Indifferent to Dolores's musings, unaware of them except for a very vague and fleeting unease, X is in the central stairwell of the apartment house.

She is free.

She has slipped her bonds and has no idea what to do now. She looks up. She looks down. She hears sounds—roarings, clankings. She detects feral smells. She cannot name or identify them. The odors are alien yet vaguely familiar, wafting through the tunnels of time, beyond her ken.

Her ears are pressed back on her skull.

There are no treats.

Champagne. Neighbor. The two thoughts come simultaneously. Dolores is pleased to be able to make her simile come true, and instantly alarmed that if Jenny Steinem should choose this moment to use the stairwell she will see X and take matters into her scrawny, nail-bitten, proprietorial hands that so recently claimed an easy intimacy with parts of Gerald's body that were supposed to be kept in moral escrow pending Dolores's return. But how can she share these misgivings with X, who wishes to explore and may, perchance, repeat the ablutions that got us all into this mess in the first place. Down below, a human voice is shouting. Incomprehensible noise to a cat, but laden with portents for those awaiting their own Pavlovian gratification from online shopping.

The intercom! Delivery!

Waitrose, Tesco, Amazon, HelloFresh, Topshop, UPS, DHL. All of those private space invaders of the new era.

There is a loud buzzing noise.

A big door is open.

The front door. Leading to the busy road outside.

X has stiffened, every fiber alert for intelligence to explain what is happening around her. There is a rolling, bashing sort of noise and another sound from above. A screech or shriek.

"Second floor."

The neighbor Steinem. The witch, bitch. Taking a delivery. From Spells "R" Us: eye of newt and toe of frog, wool of bat and tongue of dog, sweltered venom.

X, you brindled cat, do not mew now, once, twice or thrice. Or her cauldron will bubble with us in it.

Memory functioning okay, after all.

But X has no intention of mewing. Dolores feels her fear. Noise from above and below. Hostile. Advancing. Pincer movement. She turns back to the front door, not even checking to establish whether the flap swings both ways, as the neighbor patently does. X launches herself with unheeding recklessness at the flap, head-butting her way back into captivity.

"Could've sworn I saw a cat on the stairs," Dolores hears the deliverywoman call up to the person waiting on the landing above.

"Really?" Jenny Steinem replies icily. "We'll see about that."

But the champagne cork is back in the bottle.

Frau Doktor Tremayne is invited to celebrate the successful outcome of three days of negotiations to conclude a deal for the supply of technology for the latest hybrid 7 Series saloons. The MoU covers most of the wizardry behind the central touch-screen that provides audio, navigational and road condition updates along with subprograms to enhance economical running, power conservation and the modulation of the car's internal climate. A separate program—the elephant in the techie room, so to speak; the software script that dares not say its name—provides fraudulent information to examiners in their white coats when the vehicle's exhaust emissions are tested under laboratory conditions.

Her interlocutors have haggled and wrangled and probed and argued and blocked and feinted. One has tried to get her drunk to betray company secrets. Another sought to lure her to a Bavarian hunting lodge for purposes of seduction in the forest, possibly to the same business-driven end. Dolores has maintained her composure. She has pretended to retreat from her last possible price, which she had inflated before the negotiations, and painstakingly explained all the gizmos and bells and whistles that make her offering so alluring. She has undermined her rivals' exaggerated claims and assured continuity of production from her company's assembly plants in Guangdong, Milton Keynes and Brno. She has produced the legal document for the lawyers to have one last look at before, on the fringes of the Geneva Motor Show, her chief executive and his German counterpart sign the formal agreement. She has one more night at the Hotel Vier Jahreszeiten, which she plans to spend with a room service dinner and a book. She has checked in online for the next leg of her long and arduous business trip. Her boarding pass—Club World, aisle seat—is in her purse, alongside her passport and ESTA documents for Homeland Security. She has maintained her virtue. The drawbridge of her purity, though assailed, has stood firm. Unusually in conditions of siege, she has poured cold water rather than boiling oil on the ardor of the besiegers.

"A glass of champagne?"

"Champagne or Sekt?" It is an old joke among them since the earliest days of their business relationship when one of their negotiators tried to pass off Henkell Trocken as Bollinger.

"Champagne. Echt!"

A cork pops. Liquid is poured. Fizzing and bubbling into a glass. An echo of some other event. In some other place. Corks. Popping. Bubbles. Flaps.

"*Also,* to our future cooperation and the conclusion of successful together-working!"

There is a pause, a hitch in the proceedings. Silence. Embarrassment.

"Frau Doktor? Frau Doktor Tremayne?"

She hears the voice as if someone is trying to wake her from an unscheduled nap of uncertain duration.

"Frau Tremayne. *Geht's Ihnen gut?* You are okay? Please?"

"What? Oh. Yes! *Zum Wohl!*" She recovers quickly for the toast, but for an inexplicable second she was not here, in this unadorned, wood-paneled meeting room in Munich, but in her own apartment house in London, seeing the world from ground level, knowing something was amiss. But what? Why should it be? Somehow the word *champagne* had echoed from a parallel universe. Like the froth surging from the neck of a badly opened bottle of Moët or Laurent-Perrier—the way Formula One drivers do it with their jeroboams on the podium when their bodies are finally still and safe—some distant reality had washed over her current coordinates, making her feel as if she were living in two simultaneous but separate worlds. In one world, in this formal chamber in Munich, she is centered, in control. But there, in that distant universe, something is wrong. If she is honest with herself—and who is so truthful to themselves these days that they would fit that description—she can begin to imagine why.

So now there is a third world—an inner dialectic that un-
folds below the surface of the niceties of her farewell
drinks with the automakers of Bavaria. It has been there
all the time, this galaxy, this meteor-storm of unresolved
passions. But she had treated it as a black hole, a place
that was there and not there all at once.

At first, she thought her marriage was skewed because
she was doing all the heavy lifting. She worked and earned
and traveled and struck deals and burned the midnight
oil over spreadsheets and PowerPoint presentations. She
considered CVs for new members of her team and kow-
towed to her superiors and put up with the whispered
remarks around the watercooler. Success breeds envy,
but minority success—success by ambitious members of
ethnic minorities—corrodes. And all the while she was
doing this and the money was piling up in their joint bank
account, he was home and spending it.

Then she thought she had gotten it the wrong way
around. She had been remiss. Serially. Chronically. Consumed with career, promotion, fleeting glory, appoint-
ment to the executive committee, expanding power, stock
options, mentions in trade magazines. The big profile in
the Weekend *FT*. Glass ceilings shattering. When all the
while she should be doing things like they used to, when
she was his muse, his soul mate. Homework. Little dinners en famille instead of salvers delivered by liveried
flunkeys who could barely believe that they had finished
up waiting on a woman of color. She had been unfair. She
checked his credit cards and accounts. True, there was
nothing coming in from his publishers. But everything

else seemed accounted for. Maybe the fuel bill for the Range Rover was a bit OTT. Maybe there were some cash withdrawals that were something of a puzzle. But you could not spy on genius. And there was no doubt that he was a genius. You couldn't analyze creativity on an Excel spreadsheet.

But how could she synthesize these propositions? After this trip, maybe there would be a way to reshape the agenda, the SOP. She would crank it back, delegate. Send underlings to do the grunt work. Like her bosses sent her. Just one last push from her current mission: the big one in Detroit after yet one more long haul from Germany. Then home. Hearth. Matters of the heart.

There is a fleeting memory from before she left home.

Unusually, X, the family cat, has jumped up into her lap, just as Dolores is considering how different life would be without frequent-flyer phobias, airline angst, business-class blues. The cat is, generally speaking, much more aloof, refusing to seek the warmth of human contact. Dolores is slightly concerned that her elegant traveling suit will be covered in telltale cat hair, requiring attention with the adhesive roller kept by the front door, used most frequently to remove traces of errant pelt from the girls' school blazers after they have chased and grabbed the cat for a cuddle. But this time it nestles and cranes its head upward. X's blue eyes fix Dolores's brown eyes with an unusual intensity, and she reciprocates with an equally piercing gaze. Later, she will think of one of those moments when one person stares at another interrogatively and the object of that look offers optical encouragement to proceed. Like people on a first or possibly second date.

It is not clear to Dolores who has initiated the process. An invitation has been made and accepted. With their gazes locked together, something passes between them.

What nonsense, she remembers thinking.

eleven

She was, as suspected and for the record, FYI, *entre nous*, nudge-nudge, wink-wink, a natural blonde. I have her phone number but she does not have mine. She knows my name and address—I must be getting careless—but she has accepted the argument that, as a single parent and creative novelist, I require an occasional muse rather than a permanent companion. She has had a happy outcome. A walk in the park has turned into a roll in the hay with a literary figure. Major? Minor? Already forgotten? Does it matter? I have planted a tiny seed of self-reproach that her actions qualify her as a home-wrecker. We shower together. One thing leads to another. We shower again. She lets herself out, on track, I assume, to return to her day occupation as a student of art and her night job waitressing in Soho to help finance the living costs of the course gifted to her by doting parents. She lives in a flatshare in faraway Fulham, she has told me, and has traveled across London in quest of a breath of fresh air. Will she tell all? I doubt it. The tabloids would not be interested and there is no prospect of her tittle-tattle filtering back to the school-run set.

I open the studio windows to air the place. Can I really have done this? Double-deception? Betraying wife, mistress in one day? Betrayal, of course, is the inherent peril of love, the worm in the apple. Think of all those literary figures whose souls are tortured, and how often is deceit the source of the self-flagellation? Humans are frail, led by random encounters and physical urges. It should stop when the kids arrive on the scene, but it doesn't. Swans show far greater commitment to monogamy than humans do, without the vows and contractual safeguards of wealth in the event of separation. You see them on the Highgate Ponds. The female warms the eggs, the male patrols, protects—no pursuit of paramour swans or wayward geese or horny little terns for him. The eggs hatch, the cygnets arrive, gray and sweet and fluffy, and the parents bracket them in regal procession around the earthly feeding grounds. Royal game, of course. And better behaved than most of the Royal Family.

So why am I more a cuckoo than a swan, laying my eggs in foreign nests? No wonder *Marriage* is stalled. My stamina, my creativity, has been diverted into the rut of physical passion. The juices flow as the libido demands. There is nothing left for words on screen. No time. No energy. Still, I am quite pleased with my continued ability to perform on demand.

When we met, Dolores and I, it seemed different. She wasn't like the others. She didn't do any of the drugs I was selling. Definitely a plus! She didn't put out. Not an unambiguous plus, but all the same alluring, attractive.

The virgin bride. And of course she possessed the knowledge of literature over the centuries. I was clay to be molded. Clunky, obdurate clay, perhaps. But good northern loam awaiting her touch to transform this rough patch of weed and nettle and thistle into a beautiful, landscaped garden.

It can't have been easy for her. My education stopped at sixteen when I went to work to feed the family after Dad went AWOL with a lady bus-driver-whore-bitch from the depot where he was the chief mechanic. That came as a shock to all of us. And to Ma especially, of course. Five mouths to feed and no job. In those days, up in the northeast, all the old work had gone—outdated, outsourced, overtaken, globalized, sold off by the fund managers and sundry crooks of the south. Ma had such a thick accent that they laughed her out of the line of call-center job applicants. She had no head for computers. All she'd done was build a life in a rented row house around Pa and me and my brother and sisters—all younger, traipsing to school in their worn-out, hand-me-down blazers with the patched elbows and frayed cuffs. And Pa off somewhere on the bus driver's pension, living it large in Benidorm. He sent us a card once, to us kids, saying we were welcome to come for a holiday. No way, Pops. We burned the card, ceremonially. Not even return to sender. Just a dad not known to any of us since the Pa who accompanied us through Christmases and birthdays and holidays on caravan sites in the Lake District, first bicycles and games of cricket in the park, and parents' evenings at the crummy schools and breakfasts sizzling in the pan with bacon smells filling the house the morning after the payday binge—that Pa—had just fucked off. Pa became a memory. And a painful one at that. Without telling the others, I scrambled enough cash together to go and visit to try to persuade him to come home. But just going to Benidorm was a humiliation, a reminder of his betrayal, his abandonment of Ma. All the sunshine and the cheap living and the flowing Rioja—not to mention the sight of him and his floozy together—just reminded me of the crap he had left for us: social payments and shoplifting at Lidl.

"We're still family, son," he said.

"No we're fucking not."

I became a breadwinner, surreptitiously since Ma needed the benefits money, too, so we couldn't tell them at the job center that I was, to all intents and purposes, an undeclared apprentice, working for the local plumber-cum-carpenter-cum-electrician-cum-handyman. Cheaper for cash, luv, we'd tell our customers. No VAT. No HMRC. No name, no pack drill. Just wads of grimy notes, stuffed into grimy jeans. And, removing or maybe not removing said jeans, depending on the haste of the moment, the occasional cliché shag that replaced my cherry innocence with the twisted cynicism of the lothario. Lust on demand. Lust like the first, most enduring drug. Even before the local pot dealer spotted the potential of my white van cover as mule and delivery boy, I was addicted to gratification, conquest. I could never look at a woman without wanting her. And they knew. Some inscrutable signal sent the clearest of messages about what I was offering and what I was not, about the utter dishonor of my intentions.

Until Dolores came along.

A cut above the rest in every way. A person of color. A different accent. Posh. Southern to my northern ears. Beyond availability. No known boyfriend on the scene. Library-bound. A swot. And, when I dropped by to supply her roommate with E and Charlie, surprised that I could also drop names from the books I had devoured—broadsides from the literary cannon in the siege of love. Ugh! I had read my D. H. Lawrence. I had lived it. I was the gamekeeper to all those lost souls in council flats, and semis in the suburbs and big, nob houses on the hill with their broken ballcocks and manky fuse boxes and rotting window frames. Not that she saw it that way. I tried all the names I could think of—poets and novelists, Eliot and Thomas, Dickens and McEwan. I knew she was interested and I knew she would not easily admit it, to me, to herself. Why would she? She was on track for the limelight. You could see it. Study, study, study. Postgrad course already booked down south at some fancy place on Regent's Park. Then where? Business? Banks? Industry? Software? Hi-tech? Something brilliant for sure. And what was I? A drug dealer in oily jeans with a patina of paint on my steel-toed boots. A handyman good for freeing drains blocked with condoms and tampons and cocaine-tab-wrappers and dope baggies. Fused lights? Windows smashed in drunken brawl? Car won't start? Itch needs scratching? Call for Gerry. Gerry Jones. Changed by deed poll to Tremayne when Pa left. Gerry the smitten provincial who read Baudelaire in translation and pined for his own black Venus. Gerald Tremayne, with a head full of strands and ideas and words and plots

and characters swirling around for a Geordie trilogy—
Birth, Marriage, and *Death* in a family not unlike my own:
broken, fucked-up, dysfunctional, betrayed, belittled,
shamed, humiliated, normal in this England about to go
to war as a stooge of the Americans. Choose your own
epithet or era. Treachery cuts across the aeons, poison-
ing its victims from womb to tomb.

I was there, in the background, when she went up on
stage to take her degree. Her parents were all dressed up,
proud as punch—African dad in a sleek, gray suit, English
rose mother in floral dress and wide-brimmed hat. I had
put on clean jeans and a button-down shirt and a soft
jacket made of cashmere from the Oxfam shop. I'd even
been to the barber's shop for a haircut. I lurked and loi-
tered, watching from the standing room at the back of
the great hall as she went up in her gown and mortar-
board and took the rolled paper that made her a bachelor
of arts. There was a week left before she would pack up
and go and leave my life forever unless I did something
about it. So I introduced myself to her parents and tried
to flatter her dad and smiled at her mum and extinguished
the come-hither glitter. I offered her the latest printout
of *Birth Zero One.* I offered her a lift to London, saying
I'd planned anyhow to drive down that day because of the
Cup Final at Wembley. I touched her arm as I made the
pitch and saw the realization dawn in her eyes that
there was a physical me, just waiting for the word. And, to
hasten its arrival, I cleaned up my act and hosed down my
van and fitted street-legal retreads from a dodgy scrap-
yard and threw away the mattress I kept in the back. I
tidied my racks of tools and went to my supplier for the

deal of a lifetime that took up a good chunk of my savings. And I gave the rest of my cash to Ma and told her I'd be back but I had to just try my hand on the wider stage.

"Just like Pa," she said. "The acorn doesn't fall far from the tree."

"I'll make you proud, Ma. You'll see." It was the litany of the generations born anywhere north of the Watford Gap on the M1 motorway: go south and prosper. Streets paved with gold.

But she was already too choked, dabbing at her eyes with an old apron she wore—as if, I swear, she was looking for a part in *Coronation Street*.

I said farewell to my brother and sisters and told them I would send money every week for them and keep in touch—the only promise I did keep. Don't be like me, I told them. Don't give up on school. Go to university and get degrees and good jobs and look after Ma like she's looked after us.

"What's so special about this girl?" my brother said. "Is it because she's a darkie?"

It was the only time in my relationship with my siblings that my arm came up and my scarred knuckles bunched for the lightning jab and hook of the street fighter.

"I'll take that as a yes," he said, facing me down, daring me to strike.

"I love her," I said, lowering my arm. "That's all. She's the one."

"And Ma? And the rest of us? Are we just scum?"

After Pa left, they had looked to me as the head of the

household, the anchor. But, like some vessel pulled free of its berth by turbulent tides and irresistible currents, I had slipped my moorings, drifted into choppy waters with no chart or sextant or satnav to find my way home.

So here I am now, showered and spruced, sluiced clean of betrayal. At least Pa was honest and went where his heart took him, if that is what it was. I have stayed and shat in my own nest. I have allowed the your-place-or-mine spangle to return to my roaming eye. My moral compass has been warped by availability and opportunity, spinning giddily from north to south to east to west. I know it will not end here, with this latest one or two. Or three or four. How many? I lost count years ago. I look at my beautiful daughters and ask myself why I would jeopardize their well-being, their souls, their future. I think of my beautiful, passionate wife who trusts me and works to keep a roof over our heads, and love in our homestead and a future before us, and holidays in Alpine and Mediterranean and Caribbean settings, and I ask myself: why would you risk losing them for some chance encounter while you are trying to murder the family cat at the behest of a crazy neighbor, in a studio paid for by an errant French countess who might return at any moment? When I put the question like that I am taken aback by the extent of the huge web in which I have tangled myself. But I have no answer.

Right at the beginning, when we first moved south, I remember telling Dolores: "I will never let you down"— the most self-indulgent, touchy-feely of promises, the warm pledge of constancy, predictability, trustworthiness. Perhaps I meant it at the time. But I translated it into something else entirely. "I will always let you down. But I will never let you find out"—an altogether trickier proposition.

How on earth have I gotten here?

I am supposed to be a novelist but words elude me.

I am supposed to be faithful and true but I cannot do that, either. Why why why?

I have no answer to that, either. Except, of course, that the blame is not mine exclusively. Resisting temptation is not my strong suit. We met and married as equals. Now I am housebound, house spouse, househusband. It does not matter how often I tell myself that, in these modern times, there is no shame in that. It is a badge of honor to push the stroller with its all-terrain tires and disc brakes. It is a proclamation of manhood to wear the chest harness bearing the bairn, to load the marsupial shoulder bag with diapers and bottles and lotions and wipes. The very notion of the male breadwinner is an anachronism. The school run is asexual. Soccer moms. Hockey pops. The Range Rover is my mobile kraal, protecting the young from predators lurking below the mopane trees of Gospel Oak, the wait-a-bit thickets of South Grove.

Except that some ancient gene tells me it is not so. Does this gene come from my feckless father? Is it leeched from the stained soil of the northeast, seeping out from the tombs of mines and shipyards, where men in their flat caps toiled and delved, and women span and raised unruly broods of snotty children on diets of suet and tinned beans and medium-sliced white Wonderloaf smeared with Stork margarine and sliced Spam fried to a crisp in gobs of molten lard? I suspect, in fact, that there is nothing geographic in this gene. It is just as likely to be transmitted in posh southern mansions where tea does not mean supper and people say lavatory, not toilet, sofa, not couch, and make jokes about poor people nosing the brie; or in palm-shaded Mediterranean villas where the foie gras is washed down with sipped Sauternes. It is the gene that says: I am a man and men do not do women's work! Men left alone will find mischief.

Men left alone are walking time bombs.

Dolores's business trips just got longer, more convoluted. Her office hours extended into nights so that he became chef and storyteller and dishwasher and bottle-filler. While she traveled on business, in business class, he became the hunter-gatherer of the Waitrose shelves, the Top Shop lines. How, when, was he supposed to write? His day was set to the metronome of devoted parenthood. Tick, school. Tock, home. Tick, laundry. Tock, making the beds, de-turding the cat litter, buying lightbulbs, cooking suppers. Paying the cleaning lady to do the few tasks left over from his labors, his toil with the homework and the pots and pans at suppertime.

Not chicken and chips again, Dad!

It were good enough for me. And we never 'ad peas as weren't mushy!—a northern accent that he affects now for effect, beyond his adopted, imperfect southern modulation.

Sometimes, on Saturday mornings, at the farmers' market on the state school playing fields, he would espy a famous, Booker Prize–winning novelist buying his earthy organic carrots and leeks and fresh turbot and scallops. But that was Saturdays. What happened the rest of the time? No one, surely, no other artist, found his days so salami-sliced by the requirements of the brood.

And, if writing was out, how else was he expected to channel the creative flows? Was that what they meant by the objective correlative?

Gerald Tremayne strode across the road, ran up the stairs to the apartment three at a time, and noted that the treat on the frame of the cat flap was gone. Maybe, finally, X had disappeared and, with her, at least part of his potential downfall.

Then she materialized from nowhere at the corner where the vestibule met the passage.

Gerald retapes the flap so that the girls will not suspect perfidy. He picks up the keys to the school-run 4×4, needed to navigate the treacherous slopes, the dirt roads and bush trails, the swollen river-crossings and slicked mud slides and snowbound passes of Hampstead High Street and Highgate Hill.

"Still here, X?" His voice sounds a bit like a snarl.

"Well, not for much longer, buddy. I promise you that."

twelve

Where do flat-cats go at night? Or when humans leave them to their own devices during the day in that expanse of time between hurried breakfast and evening Chardonnay? Emancipated cats roam. They prowl along the tops of walls and sprint from foxes and get run over and disappear and adopt new families who put food out for them. They stalk sparrows and voles. They mate with operatic anguish, disregarding bloodlines, pedigrees, household budgets. Black ones cross people's paths and leave bipeds wondering whether that means good luck or bad.

X prefers to sleep. Day, night, whatever. Whenever. Deep sleep with the occasional twitch suggestive of impenetrable dreams.

She has identified designated locations where she takes her naps, perhaps according to the position of the sun, or dictated by the inner clock that ticks to the rhythm of her bowl being sprinkled with pellet resupply. One route takes her past the defecation box. Another leads to secret positions below human sleep-pads. An array of potential places combines two key strategic elements—comfort and security—within ear-range of sounds whose sequence and nature alert her to the impending presence of bipeds: a key in a remote lock, a footfall outside the great barrier, now breached, the faint rumble of a 4×4 pulling into the garage. Only in the small hours, when her liberated brothers and sisters crisscross the dark undergrowth and cropped lawns of the communal gardens, does she move silently from room to room, checking on the regularity of breathing, the snuffles of dreams whose secrets are unknowable. In human terms, she is the night nurse, patrolling the wards, alert for the final rattle.

Dolores is fighting this ingrained behavioral pattern for all she is worth. When X curls and settles, the inner part of her that is her mistress imagines herself with eyes wide and whiskers a-tremble, propelled by curiosity. X finds these urges unwelcome but not always resistible. Hardly has she seemed to snuggle down than she is up again, exploring. But why? There is no sign of food-bowl replenishment, no alarm reaching her from the staircase or the Chubb locks. Yet she has risen, sliding along the skirting board of the vast central tunnel of her prison, easing past the door that leads into the room of the younger humanoid playmate. She leaps onto a bed. Her paws are silent, the landing soft. No one stirs.

She is searching. For what, she does not know. She snuffles, sniffs. Jumps down from one bed, up onto another. Down again. Across a carpet. Up, now, onto the device that becomes a human sleeping bed when it is not a place for them to sit. And there it is. Whatever it is. Behind a soft, stuffed thing that she is pushing aside with her head. The flat shiny toy. But inverted, its glassy surface facing downward.

X rolls onto her back and pushes her front paws underneath it and tries to lift it, like an Olympic medalist struggling with a bar of enormous weights. She succeeds. But only partially. The object—cold, smooth, silvery, with faint odors of human fingers—is still horizontal, lying at the base of the vertical rear plane of the sitting place, its reflective face with the weird symbols still hidden. Time for the head. To push and nudge again. The shiny thing reaches the vertical. Now she sits before it. She peers at it. It tells her nothing. It has nothing to tell her. It is inanimate. Its flanks do not rise and fall to the beat and swelling of heart and lungs. It has no relevance to her. It is part of the biped world, as useful to a cat as a violin to a slug, though she does not know what either of those concepts entail. But something inside her does. Something inside her is peppering her with whispered instructions just beyond her range of perceptions, telling her to do what she does at windows, to wave to the world outside like a circus animal. (What she is really saying when she does that is: help! set me free! I am imprisoned by bipeds.)

But why should she do that? Who is telling her to do that? What would it achieve? Who cares?

Enough already. Enough work and obedience for one non–sleep cycle.

She plops back into repose mode. Tailed furled. Head tucked. The shiny toy, now in the vertical plane, rises above her in delicate balance between opposing gravitational forces, and she, secure in the horizontal plane, snoozes at its feet.

Fuck fuck fuck. Wake up, Dolores shouts. Please, X. WAKE THE FUCK UP!

But there is no sound that resembles these words or indicates that their message has been received. There is only the almost subsonic purring that turns her entire body into a basso profundo echo chamber.

Tonight, ladies, pasta!

We had pasta last night.

Just joking. Burgers. Fries. Onion rings. Ketchup.

But Mom says we aren't allowed that more than once a month.

Right. So what would you like? Linguine alle vongole? Tournedos Rossini? Coquilles Saint Jacques à la Normande? Geschnetzeltes mit Rösti? Crispy fried Peking duck with all the trimmings and hoisin sauce? I know. How about chicken and chips?

Not chicken and chips again, Dad!

They all laugh. They tumble through the great barrier and I weave figures of eight between this mobile thicket of soaring legs, cloaked variously in white knee socks and faded denim.

I like this moment. The larger male biped—who provokes faint memories of generalized hostility without a specific cause—maneuvers devices that produce liquid and steam in the section of the humanoid prison where feeding substances are prepared. (And where my bowl of unchanging pellets is left for me.) The smaller females drop heavy burdens onto the base of their sleeping box and turn their attentions to me, scratching the top of my head and massaging my neck and rolling me onto my back to rub my abdomen. I reward them by allowing them to manipulate wands with bright ticklish things that they wave in the air and I indulge them by jumping for them. The things we do for bipeds without their realizing who is in control.

Or, at least, that is how it always used to be. Sometimes there are fleeting images of a time beyond recall, when my magnificent bushy tail is no more than a root, and my energies are boundless. It was a time, though I cannot know how, or know how I know, when my instincts and needs ranged over a wide gamut of demands—for food, sleep, play and something I never had before the journey to the bad-smelling place where bipeds in white perform painful acts. It was a time before I became a secondary attraction among those who share this vast cavern with me. Before the shiny metal things arrived and the squeals of delight were transferred from animate kitten to inanimate object.

There is a moment, of course, when the junior bipeds devote some small attention to me. But I sense their interest has waned. Their brows furrow now as they peer into the silver things, large and small, stroking and tapping. What are these impostors, these insurgents? They cannot jump or bite feathers or chase tiny red dots of laser light. They are cold. Like me, they respond to soft caresses, but they require no pellets, no chamber of defecation. They sleep when the junior bipeds are not there, and awake—unlike me—on demand. As the junior bipeds pore over their new companions I peer over their shoulders. Some things seem familiar. Noses. Hair. Teeth.

Mysterious replicas of the junior bipeds with other humans displaying signs of contentment through bared fangs that, in my world, send just the opposite signal.

With a jolt Dolores Tremayne recognizes her human self through the eyes of a cat, fuzzy, incomplete. She tries to steer X closer to the procession of images. Words bounce around randomly in her feline head, as comprehensible as hieroglyphics. Facebook. Instagram. Snapchat. Her children are checking their messages. Her husband is in the kitchen, sexually sated, cooking some meal that comes from a supplier of raw ingredients and recipes who delivers once a week. And who else delivers to his door? Who delivers what during her absences, perhaps even before them on those few occasions when she is technically "at home"?

Not that a royal standard flutters over the apartment house in the style of Buckingham Palace to signal her presence to an adoring nation, still less to deter trespassers on her turf.

When the human Dolores was growing up, she had learned all about the monarchy and the queen and her ministers who offered her father sanctuary after his release from prison "back home" and his subsequent clandestine flight north, across African lands in the earliest days of the continent's independence when that same monarch—or her representatives—presided routinely over the lowering of Britain's banner and the lofting of new standards emblazoned with the colors Africa favored to show the blood of the martyrs, the mineral wealth, the riches of the fertile land and the skin color of the people, sometimes offset against an emblematic spear, or AK-47—the facilitators of freedom. Her father, Stephen Nkandla, was the son of a pastor in Zululand who taught him his reading and writing from works of Shakespeare and the King James Bible. But that same dark, leather-bound tome with its gilt cross on the cover taught him other lessons about a freedom fighter called Jesus of Nazareth who sought a new order and performed miracles to implant it and walked on water and fed the masses with loaves and fishes. The sightless blinked into light. The crippled danced. Things changed. Lives changed. For the better, as they would in his own land if he only listened to the entreaties of the many apostles who came on secret missions and recruited him as their eyes and ears, standing watch on street corners to signal with a wave or a whistle the arrival of the security forces who might disrupt the planting of explosives in electric-power substations and oil-from-coal facilities. Had the outsiders considered this consequence of their actions when they came uninvited to his forebears' lands, offering the Good Book to capture minds, but forgetting that its epistles and parables bore a message of sacrifice and renewal, of rising again? In his parallel life—pastor's son and apprentice guerrilla, the teenage Stephen Nkandla won a place to study theology at the University of Fort Hare. But just before he packed his trunk to embark on his further education, and just after an explosion that went badly wrong, the police arrested him, citing various items of legislation designed to suppress communism and forestall terrorism. He was tried—as if there was any chance of acquittal!—and jailed and sent across a short choppy stretch of water from the mainland to serve his sentence. And, after his release, his comrades spirited him out of the country by circuitous routes through new nations tasting the first flavors of their freedom. By the time he arrived in England, of course, his spell on Robben Island had brought him into contact with precisely those same people the authorities did not wish him to meet but who chose him, with his effortless English and plausible, mission-boy manner to be their voice among the well-meaning and outraged liberals who would support the movement from afar. "Our struggle is peaceful," he would tell the English people, such as his wife-to-be, who attended the meetings and discussion groups and fund-raisers. "But as our great leader has said, it is cause which we live and are prepared to die." Blending BBC enunciation with the fervor of his father's pulpit, his words—his sermons, as he thought of them—thrilled his audiences. Even the potential infiltrators from the British police special branch had to admit that he seemed somehow more credible than their contacts in the enemy camp, in the embassy on Trafalgar Square who fed them snippets of disinformation and sought clues about the next shipment of arms to be smuggled south. Stephen had fallen deeply in love with Dolores's mother, Jane Duckworth, a trainee nurse at the Royal Free Hospital and fierce supporter of the struggle for justice in his faraway land. He had persuaded her to join the organization. He had coached her in the finer points of ideology. He had introduced her to some among the comrades whose missions and activities were far more covert than his. And he had fretted for weeks after she volunteered, without seeking his advice, to head south under cover as a tourist to take delivery of a satchel of stolen documents showing the design and layout of the nuclear power plant at Koeberg, near Cape Town. He knew such excursions were fraught with risk. The enemy had spies and moles everywhere. It was quite conceivable that the whole expedition had been set up as a provocation to demonstrate the implacably hostile and frankly murderous intentions of the freedom fighters. And, indeed, Stephen was extremely relieved, though not surprised, to learn that long before his future wife was scheduled to meet with the handlers who would arrange the transfer, the trap was sprung. A hapless undergraduate from the University of Cape Town was photographed and arrested taking receipt of a sheaf of bogus paperwork stamped "Top Secret" and, in Afrikaans, "Hoogs Geheim." The case went quickly to court. The movement was held up to ridicule. When Jane Duckworth returned finally to London, Stephen Nkandla knew that she was not simply the love of his life, but a loyal and true servant of the struggle. He insisted on a church wedding—a nod to his father and to the freedom fighter called Jesus—to sanctify their vows and Dolores was not long in arriving soon thereafter, the object of deep adoration and the repository of her father's frustrated ambition to do well at college and make a mark in the world from which his ancestors had long been excluded. When freedom came, far to the south, Stephen transferred his office from a dingy walk-up in Camden to the imposing and newly liberated embassy in Trafalgar Square that had for so long been the enemy's headquarters and was now the very emblem of Africa's greatest triumph.

"We must not squander the fruits of victory," Stephen would tell Jane as they doted on their only daughter. "Our daughter will have everything we did not."

But, for all the wonderful educational advantages bestowed upon her as her legacy from her father's struggle, Dolores cannot teach X to read. She cannot produce a *Hamlet* or a Gospel according to Luke to make words make sense to the feline mind that has become enmeshed with her own. Sometimes, by acts of supreme concentration and will, she propels the furry body that she has come to inhabit in the direction of her elder daughter's iPad (John Lewis, £148.50) and maneuver her small, bewhiskered head at angles so that perhaps her new eyes will recognize something of whatever Portia is tip-tapping. It is hard for X to follow. There are hints of comprehension, without the fluidity of literacy. Why should there be? She is a cat. But she is a cat with a human heart, soul, mind, spirit—who knows?—locked inside, screaming for the sympathy and attention of a world that X interprets only on her own terms of sleeping corners and hiding places and food containers and dark zones of utter privacy. And how can Dolores interpret all these other inputs—sounds, smells, data transmitted by whisker, tail? The biped living cavern is an echo chamber that X categorizes by range and peril, but which Dolores would classify by activity and function—curses from the kitchen, and whispered giggles closer to hand, and the distant rumble of cars and buses that X hears coming long before humans do. Supper is being cooked. Her cherished iroko wood surface is probably being destroyed by heat rings and scalding spillages. Her nostrils detect odors denoting experiences denied to X—oil (burning slightly), tomatoes (chopped), garlic (crushed), meat (burning more deliberately). Other sounds: a cork from a wine bottle, the slosh of Sauvignon Blanc in a big, early-evening-in-the-kitchen wineglass. Heat. A lid prized from a pot. Steam.

A sudden insight into the chaos on the screen, a brief moment when the squiggles and ciphers coalesce and make sense. As if a curtain is pulled aside and immediately closed, X recognizes a pattern she can decode without knowing its meaning.

X can recognize letters! But she cannot understand what they say. Once, on an educational outing, Gerald and Dolores took their daughters to Bletchley Park, the wartime secret intelligence facility fifty miles north of London, to show them the origins and uses of math and computers. They had processed through the exhibits, the memorabilia, the snack bar, the mandatory shop. They had peered without much interest at the clunky Enigma machines that the British had captured and used to track German orders and deployments. To protect their insights into the enemy communications, the code breakers disguised their decryption of battle plans as reports by fictitious agents in the enemy camp. The biggest secret of all—which had to be protected against all likelihood of detection by the German intelligence establishment—was that German secrets were not secret at all as far as the British were concerned. The family had attended a display of the Bombe—a brilliant early computer that clanked and clunked its way through the jumbles of hitherto unbreakable code. Of course, its power was far less than the computing oomph of the girls' tablets and their parents' smartphones. But the process—cracking one word to learn just how the Enigma machines had been calibrated on that particular day—drew a modicum of interest.

Wettervorhersage, it turned out, was the key to a rare Nazi blunder. *Wettervorhersage* meant "weather forecast." A German ship in the North Sea sent a daily signal prefaced by that single word, encoded as gibberish that would otherwise be uncrackable. According to the brochure at Bletchley, the odds against deciphering its meaning without the Bombe are 158,962,555,217,826,360,000 to 1. Almost as improbable as the chances of winning the lottery. (Almost on a par with Gerald's Amazon ranking.) Yet even then, when the Enigma machine has worked its magic, someone using pen and paper must write down the coded letters and string them together and tap them out in Morse code on interceptable radio frequencies.

The Achilles' heel.

But "Kentish Town." What is that code for? How many potential permutations of meaning can there be? The other big flaw in the Enigma machine was that it could not encode any single letter as itself—an S en clair could not be an S in code. Yet, maybe Kentish Town means just that—the place down the road where the Northern Line tube intersects with the C2 bus route. Keep it simple!

Portia's tapping and stroking creates formulations that remind Dolores of words that cats may never know.

Tube.

Meet you.

Girl just like you.

Wettervorhersage.

Okay.

The words filter through her feline synapses, neurons, dendrites, axons, bouncing around from entorhinal cortex to thalamus to subthalamus and hypothalamus. Her eyes are not designed for reading. Her vertical pupils enable her to gauge distances for a leap to seize a prey. But what use is that to her? Her food bowl does not move. It does not range the savanna or lurk in the mopani scrub. She does not need to pounce on it. There is no great annual migration of food bowls that requires guile and stealth to remain downwind. When she eats, she feels a primal urge for protection while she is vulnerable in the act of bowing over her rationed pellets. Indeed she has persuaded the kinder bipeds to stand guard over her while she eats. Otherwise she goes hungry. She forgets her schedule. She forgets many things after a few minutes but sometimes older memories of distant kindnesses help her evaluate strange bipeds. Even if she could read words they would not lodge for long.

Tomorrow.

What is that? Time is a cycle from light to darkness but it does not have yesterdays and next days and appointments and agendas.

Why, then, is this combination of figments somehow a source of unease? What are all those concepts of meeting, of specific places, of a time outside the set pattern from waking to sleeping? Where in the vast galaxy of 158,962,555,217,826,360,000 to 1 have the celestial alignments narrowed, maybe to 10 to 1 or 5 to 1 or something manageable if not yet known?

Wettervorhersage.

Weather forecast.

Meeting at Kentish Town with a stranger, a girl like you.

Meeting. Stranger. Omigod.

Where did that come from? Where has it gone?

The wheels click. The Bombe whirs. The circuits flicker and die.

Supper's ready, girls. It is the male biped.

Spag bol.

Oh, not spag bol, Dad.

Better than chicken and chips, Astra whispers.

Giggles.

Coming!

Just joking. New recipe. Butter-fried chicken with feta, leek and minted potato. Or was it chunky chicken with chorizo? Or KFC after all?

Groan.

They leave.

Their silvery screens are emitting light. They have not extinguished them. They rely on them to choose their own hours of rest.

Dolores summons all the mental reserves she can to prevent X from trotting after them in the vain hope that, this time, her diet will include some item from the biped eating platform that will be more attractive to her primeval taste for flesh, fish, wing, feather, fur. Alluring but alien. How can she understand her appetites for these warm, living, fleshy things that she has never sampled? How can you know what you have never known?

She peers at the surface of the iPad. There is an empty space at the top and, below it, a row of incomprehensible symbols. A force X cannot understand is moving her front paw over this mishmash, halting sometimes to press downward. Four times. When she presses at the bottom of the screen, something similar appears higher up in an open space. Then her paw moves higher up the screen to more pictograms. (What are they, for goodness' sake? What is goodness?) Another push.

It is as much as can be achieved.

X has decided it is time to head to the kitchen and Dolores must accompany her. She wanted to stay with the tablet and try to determine whether it had yielded up some magic words—message sent. But what was the message? And who might it have been sent to?

So there you are, X. Where have you been? Surfing the web? Looking for tomcats? Checking the weather forecast?

More giggles.

thirteen

Gerald Tremayne may have his faults but—call him old-fashioned—he is pretty tough on the internet. His daughters are allowed to use their tablets and laptops only for half an hour before dinner and homework. Their mobiles have limited data use. He has set the parental controls to shield them from premature exposure to the depravities of which humans are not only capable but desirous, and in which he personally excels. They protest, of course, but so far, he believes, they have followed his regimen. And unbeknown to them, he has their logon IDs and passwords. He does not like to pry, of course. Sometimes, it is squirmy to see the kind of crap that preteen girls commit to the cyber world they inhabit. But it has to be done. Far more than most, he knows that humans are prey to levels of unscrupulousness. He hopes they have not inherited his faithless genes. He prays they will never meet a fellow initiate in the arts of exploitation. For Gerald Tremayne knows the tricks, the buttons to press, the vulnerabilities of youth that expose girls like his daughters to bamboozlement. He understands the insecurities that turn adolescence and its approaches into a minefield of hazard. So, usually, he makes regular checks on their web traffic, their selfies, their exchanges on bizarrely titled social media sites. Sometimes he is touched by their innocence. Sometimes troubled by the gradually expanding frontiers of their knowledge and suspicions about life beyond the homestead. Sometimes, he just wants to know what kind of chit-chat they are exchanging with their distant mother on her unending journeys that leave him as a single parent with the awesome burden of protecting their fragile, tender innocence from a depraved world. And sometimes, there are lapses.

Like in the past few days when he has been distracted. Crazy neighbor. Mad cat. Chance encounters. All time-consuming. Requiring extra attention to the banality of subterfuge—the laundered sheets, the patches of plausible explanation to cover the inexplicable gaps in his daily agenda. Where were you when? And with whom? In case the questions were ever asked. Not that they often were. Dolores was beginning to seem remote, a temporary sojourner. The girls were beginning to ask less frequently: when is Mummy coming home?

Oddly, though, his wife seemed incurious about events in her absence. She returned from her trips, laden with gifts. She was passionate. Demanding even. Sometimes, he congratulated himself on the inordinate amount of time he devoted to maintaining his skills of tumescent endurance for her immediate benefit and gratification, as if his dalliances and liaisons were, in reality, merely one more form of worship of the Goddess Dolores, font of all wealth and comfort; as if his paramours were no more than sparring partners ahead of the big bout, runners to keep the pace before he sprinted for gold. He avoided innovation with her when they tumbled together on her return. Sometimes she timed her arrival in early afternoon so that they could get to know one another again before the school run. Innovation would have been a dead giveaway. Where did you learn that little trick, she might ask? Not an easy question for the errant husband. Learn what? I thought you liked it that way? From the chandeliers.

More lies.

And now this.

Rising early for the breakfast routines, Gerald Tremayne had checked his own email (he made no restrictions on his own web usage and was always careful to cover his tracks). He had almost choked on his strong black coffee.

"*Cheri*. I will be en route Kennedy/Heathrow by the time you get this. But please, come and pick me up (Terminal 5) and carry me off to our love nest above the shrink's. I will be discreet, I promise. And no one will know where I am. Except you. Until then—your lover. And landlady! XX."

Oh Christ. Oh fuck. Fuck a duck.

He tried her cell phone. No reply. Switched off. Out of credit. Number changed. Seized by private detectives working on her divorce case. Desperate for evidence of misbehavior. Who could tell? Who could ever tell with her? Would she arrive in demure diplomatic duds or raunchy rock-star regalia, sliding stilt-like on skinny heron legs through Terminal 5, swinging her tight ass through the immigration lines and the customs and the duty-free?

He checked the wall calendar. No hockey, soccer, debating society, harp lessons, cello class. For either of his daughters. They would end their school day at the same hour precisely. He checked the contacts list of his phone, scrolling through a list of likely substitutes in the run to retrieve offspring—au pairs, P.A.s, wives mostly. Despite the gender revolution and the feminist tsunami, there were few househusbands to keep him company outside the school walls, among the massed ranks of 4×4s that prowled South Hampstead and Swiss Cottage and St. John's Avenue, encasing their charges in steel and technology, shielding them from lesser beings in rickety rattletraps and fleet saloons offered as perks of the job.

Who would it be? Who could help him get his daughters safely home—or at least most of the way home—while he went about his nefarious run to Terminal 5 in response to the imperious command of a woman who, he suspected, would have no qualms, if crossed, about blowing all his alibis out of the water. She probably kept a diary, for Christ's sake. A database of misbehavior, escapades, interludes, romps and rumbles.

That was not the only scheduling problem. With his publisher's advances all spent and his spousely stipend failing to keep pace with the inflationary demands of the cocaine trade, he had been forced to look to his laurels, reaching back into his past to rekindle cold trails and contacts on the powdery routes that led from distant Colombia to the nostrils of North London. At his level of the business, there was no massive markup, but he had at least located a wholesaler further along the chain whose supplies enabled him to build a modest list of regular retail clients, serviced at various points—street corners and dark lanes, cemetery gates and car parks, anywhere free of London's not-quite-ubiquitous network of CCTV surveillance cameras—on an axis from Camden to Crouch End and Muswell Hill.

"Around tomorrow if you are?" he would ask in WhatsApp messages on a secret pay-as-you-go phone whose SIM card changed every month. And the orders would trickle in, enabling him to overcome his own supply problems. If you lived above the shop, he liked to tell himself, who could blame you for sampling the produce?

Distribution, of course, was a big issue. Not quite as big as in, say, the popularized depictions of *Narcos* or *Breaking Bad*. No refrigerated trucks or carloads of hoodlums or planes and boats or cases of bananas loaded with narcotics. Or tugboats with tons of the stuff sealed in phony bulkheads and lockers. Or septic tank disposal drums with phony panels and false roofs. But a challenge, nonetheless, to keep his business free from likely detection by the twin authorities he feared to differing extents and for different reasons—the police, and his wife.

Gerald Tremayne doubted that the overworked officers of the drug squad would keep regular tabs on him, but you could never tell when they might like to tickle one minor loose strand of the trade to see what else unraveled. Of far greater concern was the promise he had made to Dolores soon after they moved in together: his old ways were behind him, he had told her. Trust me, he had said. A new leaf. A new man. Husband and father. Responsible. Caring. Legal. I would never want to jeopardize the family status.

From the very beginning, Dolores had placed a high priority on his promise. And one of her reasons for doing so went back to the very beginnings of her relationship with her husband and her father's view of the budding romance between the undergrad and the plumber. For years as an exile, Stephen Nkandla had simply assumed that the life that had been forced upon him—far from the slums of Soweto or the high-rises of Sandton or the posh mansions of Bishopscourt—was simply his destiny, his niche in the struggle. But, as freedom had come and his beloved daughter had grown into womanhood, he had begun to entertain seductive musings about his origins and how he should relate to them. He was, after all, African, a son of Africa's soil. His forebears stretched back, at least by association, to great warriors, Dingane and Shaka. For many of his adult years, he had been unable to rebond with the vistas of his childhood in the undulating verdancy of Zululand. When he fled north, the white authorities had declared him an outlaw. If he ever returned, the cops would nab him for sure and torture and possibly try and most certainly execute him. He was no Pimpernel to dodge his pursuers, that was for sure, no Houdini to escape their lethal grasp. Sometimes, in the lonely hours of exile, as he absorbed the culture that was all around him—figuratively, though not always literally in the alleyways of Camden Town—he looked to the great poets and scholars. The closest he came to an answer was in the work of T. S. Eliot, and one poem in particular. He was, Stephen Nkandla concluded, a Prufrock of the struggle, who would grow old and wear his trouser bottoms rolled. But after the apartheid ogres fell, and the great Mandela walked free, he began to revise his self-perception. The victory back home was *his* victory. More than many others he had sacrificed and struggled and, most of all, done his bit. Why should he not now return to the land for which he pined in his secret moments as he went about the business of recruitment and fund-raising and consciousness-raising and lies and propaganda in the service of the greatest principle of all: people were born equal and deserved to live that way, whatever their origins of class or gender or ethnicity. Once freedom came, surely, he could apply for a transfer to Pretoria, set up in Africa, await a substantial pension that would see him through in comfort, possibly accompanied by earnings that, under the new dispensation, flowed almost automatically from the policies of black economic empowerment. Finally, he would touch the soil of home and rediscover his roots. He imagined himself as the *madala*, the old man—Tata they would call him, like Mandela was called—and he would bounce grandchildren on his knee and sip single malt whisky when they were safely abed and ruminate on a life well spent that had brought its just rewards.

But it was not, of course, that simple. The dream itself was arguably unrealistic, and his ties to his adoptive land were strong. His wife had clambered up the ever-shifting ladders of success within the National Health Service and had secured a high-ranking position as an administrator, overseeing several hospitals held by a single trust. She was happy, secure in her work. She felt no magnetic pull to Africa's heaving bosom. Indeed she had once lectured him on the perils of resurgent tribalism. She had never, he suddenly realized, even bothered to learn a word of isiZulu. So how would she survive relocation to the banks of the Tugela River, where his ancestors lay uneasily in their graves, calling him home?

They had their lovely home in Muswell Hill, close enough to the monument to O. R. Tambo, the revered hero of the struggle, to make it the destination of their strolls on winter mornings and summer evenings. Their jobs were secure. They did not live in fear of armed robbery and rape as so many people seemed to live back home, if home was what it still was. They were not besieged by or beholden to an extended family reliant on their largesse. Here, in London, they were in the mainstream of life. There, they would face ever greater pressures for favors and donations to cement their share of the patronage available to the formerly disadvantaged. And then there was their beloved daughter, the young Dolores, who had done well at all the schools she attended as a pupil. Apart from rare vacations "back home," she had no natural affinity with Africa.

Maybe, Stephen Nkandla began to think—without sharing these musings with his spouse—Dolores should get to know more real Africans, move in his circle of diplomats and business types; maybe—who could tell?— meet a handsome, young, uncorrupt, promising, well-credentialed South African man with whom to raise a family and build a life in the new-ish nation for which he had fought in the struggle. The dream was dashed most cruelly. When she returned from university, she had brought in tow the shifty Gerald Tremayne, introducing him to them as the love of her life, whom she wished to marry. For once, Stephen had objected. He recalled the moment vividly.

His daughter had announced that she had a surprise to unveil at Sunday lunch. The surprise now stood on the doorstep in newly pressed jeans and a freshly laundered white shirt, faking a shy smile, clutching a bunch of flowers from which the Tesco price tag had been crudely removed. When Stephen Nkandla reluctantly grasped the "novelist" Gerald's outstretched hand, he felt the calluses and muscling of manual labor. Novelist my foot, he grunted when none could hear him.

His long years in the movement had exposed him to plenty of scoundrels and he knew one when he saw one. Like his daughter, his wife had fallen under the thrall of the chestnut-eyed charmer with his literary pretensions. But not Stephen Nkandla. He knew, from the first contact with Gerald, that his daughter would be better off taking her chances "back home" rather than setting up with this *skollie*. He knew she was making a mistake. Their children—his grandchildren—would be born into a society that mistrusted people of color, and would always block their path. And just as soon as he could tell her so, he did.

"This chap. This Tremayne. Is that even his real name? Are you sure he's what he says he is? You have a great future in front of you. There are plenty more fish in the sea. You would be better off in Africa. Among your own kind. Not with this lumpenproletariat trickster."

Unusually, she argued back. What about the values of the struggle, the commitment to nonracialism? What about the natural alliance of workers and peasants? Yes, Gerald was white. Yes, their children would be what apartheid's lexicon had defined formally as "colored." As was Dolores herself, in case he had forgotten. Had he, her own father, not fought long years of punishment and exile to consign such branding to history? But Gerald was an honest man, a man of the working class, fired by the ambition to better himself, to look after his family, provide for them with his writing which would be stifled in South Africa, limited by the narrow visions of race and corruption that still drove the debate.

And look at it this way, Pa, she said, if we went the South African route you would have to pay *lobola*—bride price—for me. And how many head of cattle do you think I am worth? After all this time in the U.K., would you even know where to buy a cow? They don't grow on trees, you know. He had smiled, acknowledging her wit and her determination, but the argument was never really resolved, as family arguments often do remain in limbo, festering, denied, awaiting rancorous rebirth. And Dolores understood very well that if her husband went back to his old ways, her victory would slip away, and, with it, the respect that Stephen Nkandla had always paid her.

She had never told Gerald about any of her battles with her father. She did not really need to. Stephen Nkandla had sought out Gerald before the wedding and informed him in no uncertain terms that if there was any whiff of betrayal, of malpractice, of activities incompatible with his status as a husband and breadwinner—in short if Gerald Tremayne's behavior in any manner compromised the honor due to his bride and her family—then there would be trouble. And not just trouble in the sense of cross words and harsh reproaches. Stephen Nkandla reminded Gerald of his time during and before the struggle, of his facility with the short stabbing spear that gave Shaka's armies the edge against outsiders who came to steal the land. He recalled, too, the dark days of the fight against the Boer, when a certain facility in the use of the Tokarev 9mm pistol and the AK-47 assault rifle was expected of him and his comrades.

To reinforce his warning, Stephen Nkandla had invited Gerald to the loft of his home in North London where he kept, mothballed and wrapped in protective plastic, a leopard skin outfit with its arsenal of what South Africans called "cultural implements" that, at least in their own country, were permitted as a form of display.

There was, for instance, the cow-hide shield with the horizontal markings and, most chillingly, a club with a rounded head, known as a knobkerrie; and an iron spear, polished, honed and known as an assegai.

The same equipment had been used, Stephen Nkandla said, at Isandlwana in Zululand in 1879 when King Cetshwayo's *impis* spilled much blood among the red tunics of the invaders, inflicting a defeat that ranked as the imperialists' worst ever setback at the hands of an indigenous force—inferior in firepower, but vastly superior in numbers, guile, and guts, fighting to defend their own land, not to invade on behalf of some distant monarch.

"It could always be used again," Stephen said darkly, judging that the moment had come for a wider lesson to put the insurgent Englishman in his proper place.

"Let me tell you something, while we are on the subject, something about your place in the world."

Gerald steeled himself for the worst, but, in fact, tended to agree with the message, as if sons of northern bus drivers and descendants of African pastors shared a similar view of the metropolitan hubris that overlay the view from London.

"There are two forms of history," Stephen began. "There is history and British history. In history, twenty million Soviets died in the battle against Hitler. In British history, the bulldog breed stood alone. Even the Americans barely get a look-in. Oversexed, overpaid . . ."

"And over here," Gerald broke in, recalling the refrain from his father's tales of war as an air raid warden.

"Indeed," Stephen said with a hint of annoyance that his punchline had been so easily stolen.

He gestured at the warrior's accoutrements.

"In history there was Isandlwana, a crushing defeat for the British at the hands of indigenous people who did not welcome them. But in British history, they prefer to focus on the follow-up engagement at Rorke's Drift. A stunning victory! Of twenty-three Victoria Crosses awarded in the Zulu Wars, eleven—nearly half—were awarded to soldiers at Rorke's Drift.

"So you see, Tremayne, or whatever name you were born with, what I am saying is that we expect no honesty from the British. We expect perfidious Albion to be . . . ?"

"Perfidious," Gerald mumbled.

What Stephen Nkandla did not mention was that, throughout his adult life, the warrior outfit had been an unwelcome accoutrement, a source of inner conflict: if he was embarrassed by the idea of wearing it, he was embarrassed, too, at feeling that way, as if he were denying his roots.

His own president, a fellow Zulu, had no such qualms. Wearing his leopard skin kit, the president had married several of his wives at ceremonies that followed Zulu tradition rather than imported Christian rituals. Attired as a paramount chief, he had attended the opening of parliament and his inauguration. With the finery that distinguished Dingane and his *nduna*, the president wanted to remind the world at large that, whatever the century, the African roots could not be enfeebled, the continent would not be denied.

That desire extended particularly to forays overseas. The president had argued forcefully that traditional dress should be worn by all of his country's diplomats during state visits and other such occasions. If the British sought to impress their former subjects with ceremonial rides in gilded carriages and state banquets and plumed hats, then it was only appropriate for the visitors to offer a riposte in kind. If you insist on thinking of us as half-naked savages, here we are—semi-clad and armed to the teeth in Buckingham Palace!

It had taken all of Stephen Nkandla's powers of dissuasion to point out the downsides of the presidential proposition that a black man draped in leopard skin constituted the most potent of anti-imperialist gestures toward his hosts, a kind of sartorial V-sign.

In some ways, Stephen Nkandla could see the point. But he understood his adoptive land far more than his leader even pretended to. Not far beneath the pinstriped façade of modern Britain, ugly sentiments coursed in powerful streams. So why pander to the hidden agenda of racial supremacy by offering stereotypes from different times? For his part, in any event, Stephen Nkandla had always preferred to regard himself as more of a universalist, a modernist, a jacket-and-trousers man, uncomfortable with emblems that predated the motor car and wireless communications. He was a creature of the present, sustained by the movement's commitment to nonracialism and its eschewal of tribal distinctions. He liked tweed jackets and slippers and a pipe of tobacco. His discomfort with the shield and assegai and knobkerrie went deep. When the presidential state visits came around, he knew, he would again have no choice—like many of his diplomatic colleagues—but to resist his leader's entreaties. Like Isandlwana, the battle might well be won on one day, only to be refought the next. So far he had triumphed, but that outcome could not be guaranteed forever. And no one gave Victoria Crosses for standing up to His Excellency.

Dolores had never learned of the encounter between her husband and her father, though she was aware that—as the years went by through births and christenings and Nativity plays and sports days—the relationship between them never rose much on the temperature charts of amity. Not so much a cold war. More a tepid truce. Even without his father-in-law's warning, Gerald Tremayne understood that he was playing a dangerous game.

If he was unmasked as a dealer, a pusher, how would the girls ever maintain their life of posh school and posh sleepovers and posh friends? How would Dolores explain the shame to her bosses? Or be dissuaded from tossing him out on his heels, packing him off to Newcastle in disgrace and failure? How do you explain to the goose that you have snorted away the golden egg? Not to mention his status as an author. How do you tell your agent and publisher that you have been supplementing the nonexistent output from the silent word processor by peddling narcotics?

Somehow, it was easier to answer any of those questions if you had a reliable personal supply of your own merchandise to numb you to the consequences. A bit like the waiter, Karl, in that Bogart movie, telling Rick Blaine that he was becoming his own best customer.

But you had to be discreet. There was no sense in cruising Camden in a black BMW with smoked-glass windows, looking for passing trade. Only if you looked like a drug dealer, Gerald reasoned, would you draw the unwanted attentions of the constabulary. The trick was to be counterintuitive, to look like anything but an identikit dope peddler. As he had learned in his earliest days, you needed a cover. You needed the appearance of a definite, legitimate mission.

Since plumbing and handiwork were no longer viable disguises, as they had been at the time he first met his wife, he had hit on the idea of disguising his supply run as part of his fitness regime. Two birds with one stone. He carried his product in a rucksack, individual deliveries wrapped in cling-film—a gram here, a couple there. Nothing too ambitious or perilous (although class-A drugs in any quantity courted serious trouble). He listened to music on his headphones as he ran with his deceptively speedy loping gait between his points of contact and trade—time-consuming, of course, but who would suspect a jogger? Even one with social connections who seemed happy to meet with him for a few fleeting seconds and a handshake at the venues on his route between bandstands in the park and secluded suburban driveways. He wore dark glasses and a beanie hat, just in case any of his clients might harbor a literary bent and recognize him from his appearances at book fairs or television talk shows—infrequent as those occasions had become. But you couldn't be too careful. If a young woman on Hampstead Heath could recognize him so could some saddo clutching his grimy banknotes in anticipation of a fleeting high. It would have been easier—if less aerobic—to use the Range Rover. But then he might have drawn even more attention. The last thing he wanted to do behind the tinted windows of the V-8 steed was to fit the identikit picture of the parasite he had reverted to being.

And today, of all days, with his French connection clamoring for attention at Heathrow, was the day for his jog.

Something would have to give.

Between organizing the breakfast table with muesli and jams, cups and saucers and bowls, Gerald Tremayne set about selecting a helper among his fellow denizens of the school run, someone generous enough to step up to the plate without expecting too much in return, or asking too many questions, or constructing conspiracies and gossip from the abrupt break in cherished routine.

"Hi, Rosemary, Gerald here," he began. "I know it's ridiculously early. But I wondered if . . ."

By the time his daughters had tucked into the yogurts and granolas prescribed by their mother—and the Marmite on toast with side orders of crisp bacon he felt they needed for stamina—it was all arranged.

"Rosemary will pick you up from school today," he told them as he drove them with their satchels and music books and sports kit. "She'll get you as far as Kentish Town. Stick together and take the bus from there. I won't be late."

He had expected his daughters to protest against this disruption of their comfortable, chauffeured routine, this rare descent from the pampered uplands of the familiar.

But Portia, the elder of the two, already tiptoeing across the divide between girlhood innocence and teenage complexity, seemed relatively enthusiastic.

"Kentish Town? Whereabouts in Kentish Town?"

"Near the tube station, I imagine."

"Okay."

fourteen

It ranked as one of the prized luxuries of the job and, sometimes, Dolores Tremayne felt mildly guilty about enjoying it as much as she did. Back home, she imagined the morning chaos and bustle, the burned toast and the spilled milk, the girls demanding freshly laundered school blouses and dazzle-white knee-socks as Gerald hovered and chivvied and panicked and cracked jokes, shepherding them along as X, the cat, wove through his long legs and tried to trip him.

"Yellow card for that, X," he would say jokingly and the girls would laugh, dutifully, at this worn, familiar humor, all part of the ritual.

In her junior suite there was no such hurly-burly, no requirement to consider the needs of third parties. She clambered naked from the luxuriant folds of the massive down comforter on the super-king-sized bed; bathed at her leisure, anointing herself from the array of expensive toiletries provided by the ever-attentive management of the Hotel Vier Jahreszeiten. She stepped onto the weighing scales in the bathroom and noted with approval that her efforts in the fitness center had been rewarded with an unchanging body weight despite the business lunches and dinners; she caught sight of herself—deliberately—in the steamed-up mirror and approved the anatomical sculpture that had thus far defied age and gravity.

Dolores Tremayne pulled on the thick toweling dressing gown the hotel provided and powered up the laptop on the walnut-inlaid desk in the suite's small but perfectly formed sitting room. Before turning in she had left her breakfast order outside her door and knew that, at the appointed hour, there would be the waiter's discreet tap to announce the arrival of hot coffee, oven-warm croissants and luscious bircher muesli, borne on tray or trolley with crisp white linen. Burnished coffeepot and cutlery. Jams in dainty individual pots. Butter on little circles of hallmarked sterling silver. Thick folded napkins—or should she call them serviettes? Scrambled eggs under a shiny dome that the waiter removed with the flourish of a stage magician.

Abracadabra!

The miracle of room service breakfast in a five-star watering hole.

With several hours to spare before her connection to Detroit, she turned to her emails only when coffee had been poured and she had lightly buttered a croissant and taken a first forkful of the light-as-a-feather *Rühr-eier* that the hotel chefs did so well.

She wished she had opened her in-box earlier, for several things were amiss.

The first that caught her eye had been sent from her

elder daughter's email address—unusual because their favored means of communication on her travels were Face Time or Skype so that Dolores could feast her eyes on her children and determine from the backdrop to the conversation whether her standards for the upkeep of the apartment were being maintained—cushions plumped and geometrically positioned; throws adorning the sofa with the precision of hospital ward bedding; TVs silent within the hours earmarked for homework; kitchen displaying no evidence of procrastination with the washing-up, or of the telltale frying pan that betrayed her husband's culinary preferences. She was not, in fact, above timing her calls at moments when she could guess where her children would be, a natural enough instinct: the protection of the brood from harm in the shape of neglect, of chaos that might be expected to flow from male supervision or from cleaning ladies who sensed that the true power behind the administration of the household was absent.

But this email was different. It had been sent hours earlier and she must somehow have missed its arrival in the champagne-drinking, self-congratulatory moments of her last night in Munich. The subject line was empty—alarm bell number one. And in the space reserved for the message there was a jumble of letters that looked like those scrambled forms you have to decipher on certain websites to establish that you are a human individual and not simply a malicious computer program gone phishing.

It said this:

"H@L#P?"

She glanced at her watch. Her late start meant that her daughters would be in class by now. She tried her husband's cell but, as it frequently did, it went straight to voice mail. "Hi there. Leave a message. Be well." No name, no number. Just a treacle-smooth voice that sounded like an invitation to far more than telephonic communication and the exchange of information.

Dammit, she thought. In a few hours, a cab would transport her to the airport where she would board a feeder flight to Frankfurt am Main for a connection to Detroit. The bookings were set in stone. When her children next emerged from the confines of classrooms and music studios and sporting facilities, she would be somewhere over the Atlantic. A joke, maybe, she wondered, but Portia did not make jokes. Irony was not her style. Neither was deception. She was a serious child, whose teachers said she did not make friends easily, a bit of a loner, though nothing you could point to as psychologically abnormal. It was just that she tended to take matters too literally, to the point of gullibility. In Portia's world—a slightly lonely world at that—people were what they said they were.

While she was considering her apparently limited options, her laptop pinged to announce a message in the inbox, this one from company headquarters, sent via a server that automatically encrypted sensitive material. In capital letters, the subject line declared: URGENT—ACKNOWLEDGE RECEIPT IMMEDIATELY.

Intrigued, she clicked on an attachment and entered her company passwords and ever-updating access codes from the SecurID device issued to senior management to keep secrets away from the prying eyes of lesser employees.

"Re: Detroit.

"Please read the enclosed press release that is about to be issued by our counter-party in Detroit. As you will see, it relates to our emissions control software installed in their diesel engines, specifically the defeat device developed at their request. It is essential that you have no contact with them and postpone your visit. Do not speak to any of their executives or journalists you may know who will doubtless be trying to contact you given your high profile in recent articles. Ensure that any data relating to this device is encrypted, stored and removed from public areas of any computer you use. Discretion is essential in this matter. This message is being sent to all our executives, developers and sales personnel with knowledge of this particular software. It is not a personal reproach. Please acknowledge receipt."

Well, that's interesting, she thought. In her experience, one of the main reasons that very senior bosses were able to remain in very senior positions with very substantial remuneration packages was their ability to divert blame onto the lower levels, onto the people, like her, who performed their assigned functions well, without necessarily being apprised of the big picture. The message, she noticed, was not signed by an individual: the trail of deniability and obfuscation had already begun. She had been concerned about this particular software because, while a degree of economy with the truth about emissions from diesel engines was the industry norm, the discovery of deliberate computerized efforts to conceal the true levels of pollution bore the seeds of reputational disaster. She had said so when the big bosses completed the negotiations to develop and supply it but she had been poo-pooed. The impact on the bottom line was too big to ignore, she had been told. If we don't do it, the French will. Or the Germans. Or the Koreans. Or someone. She would need to look out for herself. When another big motor manufacturer had been caught in a similar scam, the cost had run to billions. And, of course, the hunt for scapegoats had taken no prisoners. Every catastrophe for one, the business mantra went, was an opportunity for another. So her company had been quick off the mark to develop yet more sophisticated software to feed a hungry market for deception.

"Are you sure this is the right thing? I mean, not morally. Of course. Just tactically. Strategically," she had asked at an encounter with her division chief who sat on the executive committee and collected Aston Martins for a hobby.

"Don't you worry your sweet little head about that," he had drawled in a phony Texas accent and she had been so incensed by the gender implications of his comment that she had not fought the battle.

Now she wished she had.

Now they were telling her to go home and take cover.

They'd find out what her sweet little head could come up with, that was for sure.

Before anyone else thought of it, she scrolled back in her outgoing email and found the messages expressing her concerns—and the replies telling her to simply get on with it and do as she was told. Or consider her position. She forwarded them to a personal in-box behind a firewall, initially set up to keep Gerald Tremayne's creations and drafts beyond the view of prying eyes. (He had not used it much of late, she noted, but she was glad to be able to avail herself of its protection.)

Then she clicked on the flight schedules from Munich. With a little ingenuity—and recourse to low-cost airlines that she would normally avoid—she found a connection that would get her back to Gatwick just after lunchtime. Not her favorite airport, but it had the advantage of transit links almost to her doorstep in London. She clicked, booked, entered credit card details, downloaded boarding passes to her smartphone. Hastily, she finished off her packing and called down to reception to say she would be checking out a little earlier than planned and would require a car to the airport. By the afternoon, she would be stepping from the overland train at Victoria station and switching to the tube for a quick, easy run to Kentish Town. Then the bus home. Imagine that! On her own ticket, the life of chauffeured sedans and fawning concierges fell away like a slough. It sounded like she had perhaps better get used to it. But she would, she figured, be home in time for tea and husband and children. And a nuzzle from X. What a surprise it would be for all of them.

fifteen

It had been a difficult morning, spilling over to early afternoon. There had not been many clients but they were dispersed over a relatively wide area. He should write Soviet-era spy-thrillers, Gerald thought. Servicing dead-letter drops. Running his joes. Before technology made them all irrelevant.

There had been an unforeseen glitch when he espied the Hampstead Heath Constabulary exercising fearsome dogs with sleuth-like nostrils that quivered for any whiff of illicit substances. He had been obliged to undertake a time-consuming diversion along the Ponds. Last thing he needed: some huge bloodhound leaping onto him, trembling with the scent of contraband.

"Mind if we look in the rucksack, sir?"

The End. Of everything. Marriage, career, fatherhood, family, freedom. And for what? The question was always the same. The clients were small-time, social users, predictable. The cash flow was modest. Routinely, he plowed his potential profits back to ease the strain on the family budget that would soon become apparent if he financed his consumption on the open market. Locked into the cycle of what was beginning to look ominously like what they called a habit, the only escape was to break his dependency, jettison his secret cell phone, take his cold turkey on the chin and risk the retribution of those further up the deadly chain. Even then, if he finally wrote the Big One that propelled him onto the bestseller lists, he would live in constant fear of being exposed by his erstwhile associates. As a user, you could flaunt addiction as testimony to the agony and suffering of the tortured, creative soul. Pushers generally got a worse press. It was at moments like that—when the inner illumination of his plight shone most brightly— that he most needed a quick snort to face the enormity of his predicament. All his working life he had been uneasy about this part of his portfolio. You could pretend it was harmless, but it wasn't. He had watched enough documentaries to understand the violence and bloodshed compressed into every grain of narcotics. Maybe his clientele could handle what he sold them. But how many lives got ruined by it? How close was he to ruining his own?

He pounded on, along footpaths and sidewalks, halting briefly for the exchange of anonymous cash for diluted product, cut with cheaper powder, handed over at prearranged locations. The narrow path near the big church. The spot away from the security cameras outside the library. The alley next to the kebab shop. Behind the overflowing garbage skips. A place that reeked of urine and defeat.

On his pay-as-you-go phone, he called himself Dougie.

"Cheers, Dougie. Same time next week?"

"Cheers, mate. Sure. The usual?"

In the end, he was so exhausted and short of time that he risked taking the bus home, the class-A drugs in his rucksack replaced by wodges of cash. Laughable, really. Would you see Walter White or Pablo Escobar standing in line with their Oyster cards to swipe across the electronic reader next to the driver's cabin?

"Novelist Drug Dealer Went by Bus."

"The Peddler on Public Transport."

He lived in fear of ridicule as much as arrest.

Once home, he peeled off his sweaty running gear and showered. On his rounds he took nothing that would definitely identify him—no credit card or legit cell phone or driver's license or utility bill. It was the closest he could get to anonymity in case the heavy hand of the law descended on his muscled, well-toned shoulders. He gathered together the bits and bobs of his existence in the parallel world inhabited by his wife and daughters and lovers.

He clambered into the Range Rover.

The game was in play. *Faites vos jeux. Rien ne va plus.* His world was spinning on the wheel of fortune, and no one's luck lasted forever.

After this he would turn over a new leaf. And it wouldn't be a coca leaf, either. He would clean up his act, revive monogamy, write. One last hurrah and then the straight and narrow.

He thought briefly of ignoring Mathilde de Villeneuve's demand for chauffeuring and other services. Then

he recalled the stories after her husband's fall from grace—
and the likely consequences of disobedience. Acid on the
Range Rover. Mathilde ringing his doorbell. Confrontation. Doom.

He noticed a missed call from Dolores on his smartphone, but there was nothing much he could do about it.
By now she would be aboard a long-haul flight from
Frankfurt to Detroit. Business class. Out of range. Out
of contact. Not quite out of mind.

Hot towel, madam? Champagne?

He knew this because her schedule was held in place
by magnets on the door of the fridge so that her family
could follow her progress through five-star hotels and
overnight flights in the flatbed sharp end of airplanes,
across continents and oceans, hither and thither, never
ceasing, wrapping the planet in the latticework of her successful, executive lifestyle. Transparency, she called it. But
sometimes the itineraries looked more like bragging. Or
taunts. Look how busy and successful Mummy is, they
seemed to say, while Daddy spoons out the spag bol. One
day, he thought, I will post my own schedule on the fridge
door, from drug den to boudoir. And then we'll see how
transparent she liked it to be: 0830 school run; 0930 screw
neighbor; 1030 score drugs; 1130 seduce stranger; 1420
pick up lover (Terminal 5); 1630 pick up daughters. No.
Scrub that.

There had been a time, it is true, that idle thought of his
own counter-schedule with its stations of self-indulgence
and danger gave him some vengeful pleasure, but the
more he contemplated the bookends of his daily routine,
the more he came to think that it fell far short of what he

had promised himself and Dolores. Where was the mention of an interview on Radio 4 with Mariella Frostrup or James Naughtie—those literary gatekeepers; an invite to the big festival in Hay-on-Wye; the Booker Prize short list; a movie deal with Columbia Pictures; a call from his agent to announce the outcome of the auction of his latest rights?

He was not even invited to fill in the gaps between the gigs down the road in Kentish Town anymore.

Dolores's distant presence, incommunicado at 35,000 feet, would offer some frail protection for his hectic trip to the arrivals gate at Heathrow. At least he would not be required to invent some fiction to cover his tracks—the only kind of fiction he seemed to get round to these days.

X.

Before he grabbed the Range Rover keys to embark on his errand, he had decided to dip into his stash. Then, in one more wild attempt to be rid of X, he had loosened the tape holding the cat flap shut so that, were she to escape, it would seem to be a result of her own initiative. But, as he drove away, buzzing with his product, he could not be sure that he had also undertaken the necessary housekeeping to clear away the evidence. Like people who board their vacation flights fretting about whether they had left the hob alight, or the lights still burning in a telltale invitation to would-be burglars.

Had he left the wrapper in full view on the kitchen work surface where he had indulged behind drawn blinds? Had he even sealed it properly? The questions taunted him, like secrets whispered on the outermost limits of hearing. It would not do for his daughters to return to the family apartment before he had obliterated the traces of misbehavior. There was no one he could call for help. The only living being at home was that damned cat.

If the creature was still there at all.

If it had not already sallied forth into the hostile, perilous world from which X had always been sheltered: the trucks and buses rumbling and grinding past his door; the minicabs and people-movers, whispering Uber hybrids and construction company trucks; white vans and plump bankers' sleek Porsches; howling ambulances and wailing, blues-and-twos police cars; SUVs laden with brats; black cabs with drivers distracted by their own sagas of celebrities they had had in the back and their latest mini-cruise-break to the Med. It was not, he knew, the best of plans. Especially for the final act. If it went badly, his daughters might well arrive home to the trauma-inducing sight of terminal feline smears on the road outside the apartment, red in jaw and paw.

X would be ex.

If it went badly it would be curtains. No encores. No standing ovations. No delirious reviews. No invites to Hay-on-Wye or the Booker.

The timing would be critical. But not impossible.

sixteen

I am powerless. X has taken charge, propelled by some sense I cannot replicate or imagine, let alone overcome. Gerald has left—who knows where? The school run? Surely too early in the cycle of naps and feedings that has come to replace my dainty gold Rolex as the indicator of time. There has been some kind of panic, some discombobulation that upsets animals accustomed to their routines and patterns. X has taken me to various observation points—the key intersections of the apartment whence bipeds can be tracked and potential escape routes left open. My husband's behavior since I have been exposed to it through my feline eyes has amazed, shocked, perplexed me. Are we not a happy couple? Do we not trust one another? When I am not on the road, do we not enjoy a full and satisfying physical relationship; have dinner parties; go to the movies; play with the girls; spoil them; transport them; cosset them; help where we can with the homework? And think of the holidays in Port Grimaud and Connecticut, Africa for my roots, up north for his—the Lake District, the Peak District; Derbyshire, Lancashire, Yorkshire, Northumbria, or should that be Northumberland? In any event, was their way of life not the apex of contentment? Even if his writing is temporarily blocked, are they not a model family unit?

But being a cat—being part of a cat—has initiated me into a netherworld, leaving the ground beneath our marital feet to resemble a warren with tunnels and diggings that could collapse in on themselves at any moment. Flirtation. Sex. Lycra. Since when has the great novelist owned Lycra jogging stuff? Where does he go? Why does he carry a rucksack? He is not exactly the boot-camp type. Why does he busy himself with cling film and wrappers and a set of digital scales?

Unless.

Not that.

Please not that.

X is carrying me on some enthusiastic mission I cannot pretend to understand. I am still in awe of her—our—ability to crouch and leap to enormous heights, as if on springs or fired from the barrel of a circus gun. The feline cannonball! Watch and wonder! One minute we are on the cork floor of the kitchen. The next we are on the work surface that needs so much oiling and attention that the human in me sometimes wonders why she chose it over granite or slate or Formica or anything but this fancy, dark, beautiful wood of the rain forest that shows every stain. Here we are, this time, weaving past the microwave and the coffeemaker, the olive oil bottle and the earthenware pot of implements—wooden spoons, spatulas, whisks, ladles. We teeter past the drying rack, along the rim of the Belfast sink as if we are mountaineers on a high and precarious arête.

X is only partly navigating by visual means. She is sniffing and snuffling along. Her nostrils have become her dominant guidance system. Only vaguely—at first—do I become aware of what is drawing her along to some tantalizing, new, chemical odor. Then I realize.

Rosemary Saunders was not one of those women who drove a nonsensically large 4×4 on the school run although she sometimes felt that she would be able to fill a medium-sized truck with her habitual cargo of daughters, their friends, mountains of homework, hockey sticks, swimming togs, cellos, gym kit, laptops and all the other accoutrements of a modern, if privileged, upbringing. Indeed, there were some who thought she, above all women, fit the SUV/soccer-mom demographic.

She was in her late thirties, impeccably turned out in a slightly *House and Garden*–cum–Hermès scarf–cum–Barbour coat sort of way that recalled her roots in the county set, familiar with ponies, gymkhanas, riding to hounds and, of course, real 4×4 vehicles with dented panels and mud-spattered flanks to tow the horse-box between events. She had been raised in a culture of helpfulness, of filling the days with amusement for herself and good works to the benefit of others. Her husband, Freddy, a decade her senior, was a stalwart of a venerable brokerage that survived bear markets and cataclysmic financial crashes with ineffable grace and a gift for clearing out just in time before the fire sales began. A nod here.

A wink there. A business web of old chums who knew which way the wind blew. Who were not above starting a fire sale themselves. And fanning the flames.

As a partner and spouse, Freddy shared many of her values, particularly the assumption that people like them were somehow immune to and aloof from the shenanigans that dragged the inner workings of so many other marriages into the unwelcome public glare of the divorce courts.

Both of them took a dim view of the behemoths that clogged the no-parking zones around the school when the first wave of pupils left to be transported through snarled London traffic that seemed to ease only in the term-end vacations when parents and offspring whose families boasted a certain stature and status decamped to ski resorts in the Alps or second homes in Gloucestershire or beach houses on the Côte d'Azur. (Others, she had read somewhere, decamped to weekend breaks and package deals on the Costa del Sol or the Turkish Aegean coast. And still others went nowhere at all, not even to the Gospel Oak Lido or the beaches of Kent and Essex.)

Rosemary believed that her own vehicle—an E-Class Mercedes station wagon with netting along the backseat to keep her matching chocolate Labradors, Oscar and Lucinda, in their muddy place—was perfectly equipped for the job. This morning's itinerary, however, had been arranged at very short notice. The dishy Gerald Tremayne had called during breakfast to ask a favor and she was hardly likely to turn down a request from the famous and dashing author who doubled as househusband in his wife's frequent and possibly ill-considered absences. She could hardly refuse. Any hint of hesitation might be interpreted in some quarters as a display of reluctance to transport children of color and that would never do: she would not want any malicious tongues casting gossipy doubts on her credentials as a fair-minded, almost liberal sort of person.

Still, it was a big ask, so close to the end of term when parents might be preoccupied with finagling upgrades on Caribbean flights, or pre-renting ski gear, or checking out Mediterranean yacht charters. So many things to do. So little time to look after second-home villas in the Dordogne or Tuscany, book convertible Mustangs for the Route 66 pilgrimage, tailor the dates around the salmon season and the grouse shoots. Not to mention the Serengeti migrations.

Never let it be said that I did not do my bit in the interests of social harmony, Rosemary was thinking. Never let it be said that I did not put my shoulder to the wheel.

Kentish Town, it was true, lay outside her comfort zone and familiar navigational coordinates. Normally, she would have preferred to see the Tremayne girls home and safe, rather than deposit them in a neighborhood that appeared to be populated by people whose lives had been far less fortunate than hers. Many of the people on the sidewalks gave every appearance of having been crushed by misfortune, collateral damage in the scramble for riches that deposited the Saunders of this world in comfortable, leafy neighborhoods with private schools and late-model cars and lolloping Labradors. But given the afternoon schedule—an away netball game for her youngest and an extra maths tutorial for her eldest—she had little choice but to concur with Gerald's arrangements.

Waiting for the girls to arrive, she switched the interior car-door-locking system onto automatic and scanned a dog-eared A-to-Z to work out a route. Always plan ahead, she had been taught. Surprises are not good. Unless they arrived in a pale blue box marked "Tiffany" on your birthday. She was not worried about herself, of course. In preparation for the walk with the dogs—and in light of reports in the local paper of muggers on motor scooters abroad in her neighborhood—she had switched her antique Rolex for a nylon-strapped Timex. She had left her Gucci wallet with its sheaf of debit and credit and store cards in a locked drawer on the marble-topped island across from the Aga cooker in her cavernous kitchen. Given the time pressures, it had not been possible to rearrange the dog-walking schedule, so she was still wearing her knee-length Dubarry boots and waxed cotton coat when she pulled up outside the school.

Yet, despite the possibly illusory protection offered by her retrievers, she felt a lingering unease about her expedition to Kentish Town. Oscar and Lucinda would be no match for the pit bulls and Rottweilers she assumed would be the dominant breed.

seventeen

Miles above the city, the sky is cluttered with hurtling, jet-propelled tubes of aluminum and highly flammable fluids, packed with hominids of all inclinations and identities, each seized with mounting, unspoken tension in anticipation of the bumpy descent: the screech of landing and the lurch of reverse thrust; the moment when the seat belt signs are extinguished and the unseemly scramble begins to retrieve the contents of the overhead baggage locker; the push and shove to escape the claustrophobia of the grounded craft, now so ungainly in earthbound mode compared to its avian elegance aloft; the race along moving belts and neon-lit corridors to cross the finishing line of passport control, baggage recovery, customs, scrummages for cabs, ill-tempered lines for onward transportation by train; the frantic scanning of name boards held by sad men in sad suits who drive tired Fords and Toyotas and sometimes Mercedes-Benzes back and forth between airports and offices as if bound to the tick-tock wand of a metronome. All part of a single competition to be first for reasons that none of the contestants could easily define except by saying that it is part of the human condition to hustle and bustle and get ahead and leave others behind in the daily marathon that, ultimately, ends in the same dark place for all us, with no winners or losers in the processes of decay.

Dust to dust.

X knows nothing of all this. The sky is too distant, beyond the transparent walls of her cell, where winged objects hurtle in and out of her field of vision, like gloves tossed in challenges to a duel from which, as a flat-cat, she is eternally barred and shielded. On this day, snuffling along the work surface, she knows even less. Her immediate quest for knowledge is limited to an urgent desire to identify the white powder that, initially, causes a feline sneeze and then—heavens above, Dolores is thinking—finds its way through the membrane of her nasal passages and into her bloodstream and her dainty cat's brain, boosting the supply of chemicals that bring a sense of pleasure and well-being, confidence and a yearning to finally shake off the shackles of her condition as a creature of the indoors.

Oh shit, oh shit, oh shit, a voice inside her is saying. But she cannot hear it, and would ignore it if she could.

On board the airborne aluminum tubes—on base leg, downwind and final approach, flaps extending, engines slowing, altimeter spinning counterclockwise, radios crackling with encoded gibberish in alpha-zulu-runway-five-ah-zero-roger-over-and-out-speak, transponders pinging, computers locked onto beacons—there are gradations of pain and comfort corresponding to the classes that separate passengers by wealth or connection or frequent flier points. Only two of those passengers concern us today.

They are both female. They are landing at different airports, flying in from two different destinations. There are some similarities. Both are wearing houndstooth suits in black and white check, initially made famous by a well-known Parisian couturier. Both have expensive, well-used hand luggage in the overhead locker.

Both have the look of people used to a degree of deference and respect. Unbeknown to one another, both are contemplating imminent reunion with Gerald Tremayne.

But there the similarities end.

One of the women is of darker skin than the other and seems out of place aboard the budget airline plane carrying her from Munich to Gatwick Airport south of London. She bought her seat late and was unable to secure a place near the front exit. She has just spent almost two hours jammed between fellow passengers as miserable as she was at the restricted leg room, the indifferent-to-nonexistent service, the sound of whining babies and cantankerous Arsenal fans returning from an unsuccessful joust with Bayern Munich. Ahead of her is the trudge through dank corridors, obstructed by lines at immigration and at the vending machines selling tickets on the Gatwick Express. This must be endured stoically. The only upside to the discomfort is that it has distracted her marginally from asking herself, over and over, two questions: what did the bizarre email from her daughter's account mean? And, who will be the scapegoat for the emissions imbroglio that, she has an awful feeling, will balloon into something catastrophic once it is discovered that her company played a central part in the development of fraudulent software. It is quite probable that her bosses even now, like people cheating at that game where you pin a tail on a cardboard donkey—but without wearing the blindfold that is the whole point of it—are conspiring to dump the blame on her and others in her team who were sent out to peddle the duplicitous codes. Outsourcer's remorse. Easily overcome by deceit.

The other woman has had an easier journey, surrounded by purring cabin staff responsive to her very few needs on the first-class run from New York, stretched out high above the Atlantic, remote from worldly concerns. As landing approaches she knows there will be no hustle and bustle and sharp elbows. She will be eased gently from the airplane, albeit into the cruder realities of Heathrow. She has access to a privileged line at passport control. She will not need to buy a train ticket because a handsome novelist will be awaiting her with a smile and the anticipation of intimate moments.

She has not yet decided on the precise moment to break the news to him that it is all over. The jig is up. The love-nest lease agreement rescinded in a way that will make him liable for outstanding payments. She has diverted herself by considering her options. Will she tell him before they arrive at their eyrie or later, when he has been permitted, unwittingly, his valedictory trot around the paddock of their shared passions? In her carry-on bag, she has packed excruciatingly tight jeans, monstrous platform shoes, a ragged T-shirt that advertises her sculpted bosom and a black leather jacket. En route to the immigration formalities she plans to change out of her business suit and into these other clothes. Jekyll and Hyde bis. In truth, she has an unaccustomed soft spot for this plumber-cum-writer who, like her, wrestles with origins that dictate so many of his responses. But she lives in a world of hard choices and ruthless decisions that will determine her future comfort and prosperity. Wherever she came from, she understood where she wanted to be next, and how to get there.

Late the previous night she departed JFK as the newest trophy of an eminent, if gullible and infatuated Wall Street figure whose role, she had decided, is to replace her onetime diplomat husband as her guardian, sponsor, spouse, and source of infinite credit. In her heart she knows she has not resolved the central question of where true north lies on the compass of her dreams. She requires no financial support, since her coffers have filled amply over the years through her activities on behalf of the family businesses and through the judicious deployment of lawyers versed in the twin arts of the prenup and the postnup. Yet, she cannot escape the visceral pull of perilous adventure, defying gravity itself on the high-wire of risk. In her new life-to-be she will again be the glittery hostess at homes on Park Avenue and in the Hamptons, just as she once ruled the salons of diplomacy. But potent currents still propel her into tangled, inexplicable liaisons. She will never know for sure when the call to the dark side will summon her, as it did to the unexpected intrusion of Gerald Tremayne in London. And so, for now, she has resolved that it is time to fortify her defenses. After her last-fling stopover with Gerald Tremayne she will fly on to Paris to meet with her new American beau, who is already there on a business trip, awaiting her in a suite at the George V just off the Champs-Élysées.

On final approach, she reaches her decision.

In the arrivals area of Terminal 5, Mathilde de Villeneuve will, for the last time, strut her stuff in her night-owl colors. Thereafter, she will never see Gerald again. That, at least, is her plan and, as we all know, even the best-laid stratagems may go awry.

She commandeers a cubicle in the restrooms on the way to immigration and opens her carry-on to change.

Showtime!

Dolores has no hope of restraining X.

X is flying, irrepressible. She claws furiously at the loosened tape until the flap swings wide. She thrusts her way through and, instead of following the familiar route upward, turns down toward the staircase that leads to the front door of the apartment house. She is aware of a shadowy presence that would normally persuade her to scuttle for safety. But safety is not on X's agenda today.

Dolores recognizes the figure on the upper flight of stairs as the duplicitous, deceiving, husband-stealing neighbor from higher in the block. But, along with rage, she also feels a kind of pity: Gerald's women are all in the same nonexclusive, nonproprietary boat: they all have illusions of a special, unique place in his heart, but they are all betrayed as much as she is, because his heart is splintered, a hall of mirrors, a distortion. They are all fools, and she has joined them. They are foils to his ego and his insatiable physical needs. They offer their bodies for his use alone, while he spreads his favors wherever they may land, like sycamore seeds borne on the wind. He resembles a creature in one of those wildlife documentaries when some would-be David Attenborough, or even the great man himself, must yet again explain the imperative that bonds the humping tusker and the rutting stag and the roving husband-hunter-gatherer in the central male conundrum: how can I be sure that my genes survive the generations when I have no ultimate control over the crucible of their procreation? Only the female can be confident of her own claim to parentage. The act of gestation is the ultimate validator. So the male must perforce spread the love. It is the predator's first and last line of defense.

X is poised at the big, heavy front door with its frosted pains of mismatched glass and green institutional paintwork that makes it look—to humans—like a throwback to social housing in the 1930s. To cats, of course, it is merely a barrier that may open or close to no evident rhyme or reason.

Now it opens. The postwoman—post-person? Who was the pre-person?—has pressed a button marked "Trades."

Trades!

As if it were *Downton Abbey*. Or Buckingham Palace.

The door swings open. The post-person is laden with parcels for delivery to online shoppers who scour the web for bargains on sale, or at least, for acquisitions that may be presented as such to their spouses. She steps forward, balancing her load as she pushes against the weight of the door. At just the moment when she is poised to overcome its inertial resistance, and is at the tipping point between effort and entrance, she is aware of a blur, a rush, a furball fired through her legs like a bazooka. The door, as it does, swings wide, abandoning all efforts to counter its weight. Like a duped jiujitsu combatant, the post-person finds herself pressing against zero opposition and stumbles. Packages in brown cardboard fly and fall and trip her. Biped down! The neighbor, following X, rushes toward her, and the postie thinks help is on the way, but it is not to be. Ms. Steinem—who is expecting no tribute this day from Amazon or J.Crew or House of Fraser—leaps over the fallen fulfillment operative in a single bound, intent on following X who has now scampered through the garden and is poised at the roadside, peering in wonder at a mighty red 214 single-decker bus that is roaring by.

Yes, yes, Ms. Steinem hisses. Run out into the road, you evil, condom-piercing creature. Under the bus. Under anything—Jaguar or Bentley, Toyota or Škoda or Mercedes or Ford. Whatever! Run under those treaded tires that will squeeze the bejimminies out of you.

But X turns right on the sidewalk, bushy tail high, like one of those objects held by tour guides so that their charges may keep track of them. Now she is heading south, eyes bright, an undefinable sense of purpose driving her every step.

Dear God, Dolores is thinking. This is it. I am going to die in a cat's body. I am going to be flattened on the road in a mess of fur and blood and broken bones. And when X dies will I also die, wherever I am? In Munich or Detroit or Osaka? Will my biped self simply evaporate from view, collapse in on itself as its spirit struggles free of the highway massacre? When the soul leaves the body, all life ends. It is a destiny to be averted at all costs.

She feels like one of those figures in movie animations, perched aloft some monstrous beast and seeking to steer it.

X, X, X, she screams. Listen to me! Do not leave the sidewalk. Do not cross the road. To get to the other side in response to any impulse. For both our sakes.

But X gives no indication of heeding her.

Finally, as a result of courage summoned from nowhere, she has fulfilled the destiny that generations of breeders sought to deny her. She is a flat-cat no more. She is beyond the flap, in the world where cats are supposed to be, breathing the air of freedom. The anxieties that always drove her to retreat into the family dwelling box, to seek refuge under biped sleeping pads, to mew plaintively when her pellet bowl is empty, have all fallen away. There is an urgency now. A mission that fuses her and Dolores Tremayne's sheltering instincts into one. Something of the message on the glittery pad has seeped into her cunning cat's brain. Something of the human reflex to change destiny has infiltrated her indolence.

X to the rescue!

She is a cat reborn, entering a new and exhilarating world.

Dolores recognizes landmarks to which no flat-cat may be privy. The bright red postbox. The wooden garbage bin, often fly-tipped. The estate agent, often crooked. The sub post office. The beauty salon with its offers of facials and massages. The dry cleaner. The pizzeria. The Turkish place. The bus stop.

How long will her coke-cat's buzz endure before X awakens from this drug-fueled urge that is propelling her inexorably onward, along the sidewalk, beside the hedge protecting the Heath, the tennis courts, the bowling green that is sometimes a croquet lawn, the road that leads to the farmers' market on Saturdays and the tennis courts where, in better days, she and Gerald knocked balls about and giggled with the girls?

Dogs! There will be dogs. Pit bulls. Jack Russells. German shepherds. Doberman pinschers. Lurchers. Labradoodles. Newfies. Schnauzers. Dalmatians. Weimaraners. Bizarre names—so many foreigners! From far-flung exotic breeds. All sharing common characteristics—the urge to public defecation and the sniffing of private parts; the implacable bloodlust displayed toward cats; their mammoth jaws and saber teeth and lolling tongues. No wonder we need Brexit to take back control of our canines. From now on it will be British breeds FIRST.

But X knows no fear. Of buses. Cars. Hounds. Cycles. People.

A man is coming toward them with a slobbering, snarling bulldog on a leash, tugging at its walker who uses both hands to try to restrain it. But X does not waver. She accelerates toward the oncoming creature and, quite abruptly, balletically, leaps over the bulldog, leaving it mystified: surely there was a cat on the pavement that is now empty?

Pedestrians, now, stop and peer and look at the sight of a rag doll–cum–Maine Coon flat-cat, all fluff and fur and piercing blue eyes, resisting all blandishments. Here, pussy, pretty pussy. Valuable pussy. Ransomable, reward-bearing fancy-cat. Dick Whittington redux. Driven to a place where the streets are paved with gold, along sidewalks smeared with spittle and the detritus of biped living—beer cans, fast-food wrappers. An obstacle course that X somehow navigates deftly, refusing to be distracted by the lure of strange odors, sights, temptations.

Despite herself, Dolores is beginning to enjoy the ride. Or, at least, is resigned to its outcome. Hoping it will be quick and painless. Hoping that her biped self will survive. Wondering how she will break the news to the girls. The girls who play with tablets and laptops and risk terrible things from strangers.

X glances back at the apartment house receding into the far distance, and Dolores shares the view. How odd it seems from the outside, without comforting enclosures and hiding places. How odd the outside world seems—a place of no enforced coordinates, of free will that may be translated into action, of tripwires that have no name.

A crowd seems to have formed behind them, following this strangely magnetic, magical cat. The bipeds are led by the upstairs neighbor who wants to be in at the kill. At this point in their odyssey, the pathway is narrow. A crowd of would-be fitness types has spilled out from the green fields of the Heath where they have been led in pseudo-military exercises by a man in camouflage fatigues barking orders at them. They had planned to jog the final section to their dispersal point, conveniently located opposite a public house. But Ms. Steinem blocks their path so their leader enjoins them to a form of slow advance with knees jerking high.

Hut! Hut! Wait for it! Left right left right!

Seeing this retinue in apparent thrall to a cat, others join in—a homeless person with a shopping trolley of rancid possessions, two women with double push-chairs heading initially for the Lidl shop, now, with their bewildered twins, carried along with the flow. Their chariots prevent anyone else from overtaking so the crowd grows larger, passing a school on lunch break where a mob of blazered students, desperately questing for an end to terminal, existential, adolescent ennui, joins the flying, halting, swelling wedge, using the occasion to light up clandestine cigarettes and exchange high fives. Bewildered, a clutch of schoolteachers resolves to keep an eye on their rogue charges, falling into line behind them, worried about health and safety issues if their pupils collide with buses or motorists or rival gangs. A lady in an oversized white coat and a peaked cap, who is bearing a sign that says "Stop! Children Crossing!" sees an opportunity to help and tries to shuffle along the flank of the multitude to head off vehicular confrontation.

Dolores cannot decide whether X is the fox and they are the hounds, or whether she is the pied piper of Hamlin and they are the rats. The latter seems more appropriate. Especially in Ms. Steinem's case. The ur-rat; the uber-rat; the rat par excellence with its mean little claws and toxic teeth and furtive scuttlings.

Somehow, X has crossed a road junction at a traffic light with a sign in green signaling safety to human pedestrians but offering no special guidance to her kind. Ahead there will be the Costcutter where you can return unwanted delivery items, or buy smokes and booze and milk; and the pub where they advertise real ale and Scotch eggs; and the auto body shop where they repair crumpled Porsches and dinged Bentleys; and the bridge under the rumbling railroad; the carpet shops; that funny little Italian place where they always mean to eat but never do; the medical center where humans go for their coughs and sneezes and aches and pains, their pills and potions and referrals and dismissals; the fire station—bells ringing, siren sounding, lights flashing. How can X be route-finding like this? Dolores wonders, imagining that maybe the cat has raided her home computer and downloaded the satnav software that she sells to high-end car production companies.

Heavens, she thinks, we might even make it to Kentish Town tube station. She finds herself giggling, hysterically: I hope X packed her travel card. The world's her Oyster. But where would she put it?

Tee-hee.

Gerald's fears and hopes are confirmed in equal measures when the JFK passengers begin arriving at Terminal 5. He has been prowling among the men with their signboards who stand immobile, bored, awaiting their clients, fidgety, glancing at their watches, calculating parking charges, tips, delays, traffic reports, oil changes for the

VW Sharans and Toyota Priuses wedged among the big shiny SUVs in the multidecked parking lot. Their boards identify their soon-to-be passengers by name, as if they had all lost their owners and were lining up for the hoped-for rediscovery, like stray dogs at the pound. Who were all these people whose names adorned the boards or were printed on A4 paper in large black font-sizes, or glowed from tablets? Barry Schmitz; Felicity Woodburn; Slough Ergonomics; Dominic Brown; Arthur Green; Fred White; Nelly Black; Permanent Rose. Why no Blues, Yellows, Purples? How come the evolution of names has denied the existence of Reds and Umbers, Aquamarines, Mauves? Or were there secret armies of Jimmy Ceruleans and Fanny Cadmiums and Algernon Phthalos and Shrinking Violets, too shy or poor or embarrassed to have their names on boards held by men as still as statues at Heathrow Airport? Were the tube trains and buses from the airport filled with skulking Alan Alizarins and Doris Dioxazines? Gerald had once tried his hand at painting, an ill-starred foray into a different form that seemed initially to hold much promise. He fitted the part—hollow cheeks, unkempt hair, legs in faded denims spattered with paint in colors of all permutations, Payne's grey and burnt sienna and titanium white and cobalt blue. He had painted and painted and gone to classes and painted glasses of water and gaudy flowers and ships at sea and, once, a naked woman whose olive body he felt ashamed to have insulted with his daubings. So much so that he had apologized after class. Only to be ignored. Only for the class tutor to inspect his depiction of her and whisper: "Don't give up the day job, Gerald. Not just yet."

The memory of the humiliation jars him, bounces him back to the present. How has he gotten to this thought, from the meet 'n' greet zone of Terminal 5 to the erogenous zones of a naked stranger? Was this where all his neural pathways led? Should he make a note of this stream of consciousness depravity in his old, battered, rarely referenced Moleskine notebook where he jotted ever fewer great inspirations as the moments of illumination themselves dwindled, as his muse forsook him in every way except the licentious? Or should he rather just let it float off into that nebulous Bermuda Triangle of memories never to be retrieved—incomplete, ill-formed, half-baked; the stuff of male reverie; everything channeled, inexorably, inevitably, irreducibly toward the cleft of thigh and swell of bosom that drew a man's thoughts and dreams and musings from any single starting point—you name it: a bus stop, a café, a postcard, a brick wall, Costa coffee, AP cars—to the confessional of carnal fulfillment. Forgive me, Your Eminence, for I have sinned and wish to do so again and again and again.

There was a stirring among the drivers and greeters. He sensed it before he saw her. He thought there might be a communal shift toward tumescence and all the signboards would be lowered, simultaneously and strategically, to cover the shame.

He could understand why. This time, she had gone too far. Over the top. Irresistible.

Start at the top.

Her hair was bunched up so that it looked as if she spent most of her life in bed, a great, tarty tangle of locks and scarves and beads. She had made up her eyes with mascara that flew off in points to the left and right. Her dark irises resembled impenetrable pools from which you would never resurface. Shark's eyes—deadly, unflinching, intent on the fulfillment of instinct, appetite. Bloodred lipstick. Her face tilted up like a flamenco dancer. Except that flamenco dancers did not wear worn, torn T-shirts with a V-plunge neckline, an iron crucifix; black leather jacket that was never designed to disguise the hourglass waistline; low-hip jeans tight across buttocks and crotch; and platform shoes that made her slender, muscle-sculpted legs impossibly long.

She locked eyes on his. He stood transfixed. The ranks of drivers from AP Cars and GLH and Acme minicabs and Addison Lee and Uber blurred into soft focus. The other arriving passengers became a gray featureless wave of decelerated movement. Only she had color, pyrotechnic spangles among cold coals and dry embers.

Who was meeting her, this apparition? Who had the sheer fortune to be chosen by her for what any spectator knew with certainty would follow in some apartment or hotel room or boudoir hung with silks, clothing cast aside in wild abandon? Gerald found himself grinning and struggled to compose his features into a worldlier expression. Knowing what only he could know or anticipate among this gallery of losers and no-goodniks, waiting spouses and brothers and sisters and lovers, pickpockets and spies and chancers and panhandlers, privileged to witness her swoon into his arms, the first tongue-tying kiss, the brush of her ringed hand across his bulging groin, the clutch of his fingers around her rump.

Now, they are heading north in the mighty 4×4 steed.

He asks her the time and she gives him the hour in New York, five zones away. He checks his watch for more parochial calculations. Apartment. Welcome. Fulfillment. Home before the children. Shower and spag bol. Sublime to ridiculous. The schedule will demand calibrations of speed and euphoria in equal proportions. Was it extreme risk or simple insanity? She is curled in the leather passenger seat. Her hand has rested on his upper thigh for much of the journey. Close to his true brain; the epicenter of thought, planning, analysis. But now her fingers are busy with credit card and mirror. Chop chop chop. White powder given freely from his stash. Caution is thrown to the winds. He has already partaken. So has she. They are competing for the highest high, the first cardiac tremor. He has sniffed the stuff off a thumbnail, indifferent to the police patrol car next to him in the traffic whose occupants miraculously do not espy this chemically-fueled disdain. And now she must dip in again. On the SUV's dashboard a warning light is blinking because she has unhooked her seat belt in order to deal with her class-A business, but nothing can happen to them. They are immune to disaster, set free from tawdry concerns. There is a purity in all this. A beautiful woman. A vehicle with such effortless muscle, such irrepressible verve that it leapfrogs traffic lights, surging forward unscathed as the colors change from green to amber to red. Lesser cars ahead pull over in fear and loathing as their drivers espy the massive chrome grille in their rearview mirror, bearing down on them, barracuda teeth bared for the kill. Pedestrians leap for safety as the realization dawns that the beast will not slow for them, whatever the Highway Code may say about their priority.

Westway. St. John's Wood. Regent's Park. Camden.

The lure of the tryst.

Vroom vroom.

X has moved into a higher gear. She does not know why. Her bushy tail is erect, a beacon to her followers, who are increasing in number, curious about this messiah leading her apostles south toward Kentish Town. What can it mean? Many people have joined the motley. Some even swigged down their pints in the Southampton Arms and hurried to join the pilgrimage. Among them are students; goths heading initially to stand in line for the latest wild performance at the Forum but now distracted; office workers abandoning smoke breaks, still clutching cardboard cups of flat white and latte and mocca-chocca-chino. Two video journalists checking the latest social media alerts on their cell phones have jumped off a C2 bus heading north to join the mob heading south. One of them tweets to her 27,000 followers: Weird scene at #KentishTown fire station. Hundreds follow blue-eyed #cat on #HighgateRoad. The other sends a photograph to his 14,000 followers on Instagram. Both can handle Facebook posts while loping to catch up with the peloton of bipeds pursuing the mystery quadruped. Two legs far outnumber four.

X does not look back. She does not recognize the feeling of trepidation, of looming disaster that consumes the

Dolores within. She cannot divine the nature of the magnetic attraction that draws her forward. Never a great one for sustained exercise—cats of any configuration, from cheetahs to ginger toms, rarely have stamina—she has nonetheless accelerated, upped the pace, lengthened her stride. From the front row of her new followers, she looks with her furry thighs as if she is wearing raggedy culottes. Cyclists are now drawn in and the rabble overflows the sidewalk. Police officers in a patrol car drive by in the opposite direction and call in a situation report then hang a one-eighty, keeping well back, but filming the unusual phenomenon. In distant reaches of Highgate and Mornington Crescent and Regent's Park, responding to the call, other officers hit the buttons for bells and sirens. Someone calls the RSPCA. And the shelter for orphaned animals.

Twitter addicts nudge one another on buses and comment on the strangeness of the times.

Hashtag #runawaycat.

Trending.

X is trending! Viral!

Someone calls *The Sun* on a cell phone, requesting a tipster's fee. A bored news editor pricks up his ears, recalling the musty dictum from the storage vaults of time that cats, golf and Nazis always sell vast numbers of newspapers. He senses potential and authorizes the tip-off fee. Fifty quid. Five hundred for a man-eating Bengal tiger on the loose in a Soho strip joint. But you can't have everything.

Eyeing a vast room with many empty desks from the latest round of buyouts and departures, the news editor singles out Reg Crouch, a junior reporter who has been dreaming of interviews with naked celebs, or B-list movie stars poised to leap in a suicide death pact. A couple of days earlier, the news editor had sent Reg out on a story about a parrot stuck in a tree and his reporter had bravely clambered to the rescue. Pretty Polly! The boy clearly had affinity with furry, feathered species. A big mistake.

Since Reg's photograph appeared in the newspaper with the rescued parrot perched on his extended index finger, the phone has been ringing off the hook. Who knew people had so many animals to lose? Lemurs. Ferrets. Stoats. Weasels. Rats. Mice. Hamsters. Badgers. Hedgehogs. Rabbits. Parakeets. Cockatoos. Budgerigars. Canaries. Guinea pigs. Sloths. Ducks. Geese. Teals. Coots. Baby hippos (really!). *Diplodocus. Tyrannosaurus rex* (not really!). Hah bloody hah!

LOL.

"Cat story for a change," the news editor says. "Take a cab."

"Run out of fucking parrots, did they?" Reg mutters under his breath.

"Page one if you find a Nazi on a golf cart to go with it." The news editor cackles, his chest erupting into a bubbly, wheezy emphysemic gurgle.

Nazis? Golf? The old bugger's lost it, Reg thinks. But at least it's on expenses. At least it's not another effing parrot.

X is galloping. She still has not figured anything out. How could she? She is a cat. An out-of-control, tearaway cat propelled by some crazy instinct. Dolores, along for the ride, is filled with terror. She cannot know what—if any-thing—X has in mind. With so many reasons to be fear-ful, she does not know where to begin to tabulate them.

The followers are multiplying. Ms. Steinem has main-tained pole position, despite being jostled by the mass of jogging, trotting people who struggle to keep pace with the unexpectedly athletic cat, loping like a cheetah about to switch on the afterburners. The great, bustling pro-cession is approaching a church, a towering edifice in blackened stone. Congregants pour out, raising their hands skyward in thanks and wonder.

And as X is now drawing nigh, the disciples begin to rejoice and praise God with a loud voice for all the mighty works which they had seen.

Where did that come from? Dolores wonders.

Her cats' ears pick up a new sound. Hallelujah.

Hallelujah? Dolores is thinking. Halle-bloody-lujah?

Her cats' eyes widen in amazement for—lo—congregants are laying down their coats and jackets and X is sprinting across them. It is too late to stem the tide.

"Teacher, rebuke thy disciples," Dolores is thinking. "And he answered and said, I tell you that, if these shall hold their peace, the stones will cry out."

Luke. Ch. 19, v. 40.

Luke? X wonders.

It has been one of the better days of Stephen Nkandla's career. Not on a scale, say, with Mandela's walking free in Cape Town, or the first elections, or winning the World Cup rugby game, but, nonetheless, a satisfying victory.

On days like this, he feels the struggle has not been all in vain. The grand designs framed by Mandela and his cohort, denied by venal successors, have been reaffirmed. Sanity has survived one more encounter with its adversaries.

The tussle—a rerun of so many earlier skirmishes—had been with his immediate boss, the high commissioner, who is a close ally of the ultimate boss, the president back home. The high commissioner is his de facto viceroy at the Court of St. James's and operates with the implicit weight and gravitas of presidential authority. Sometimes, Stephen thinks, she believes she is part of the president, a remote but organically identical expression of his will. Like in those sci-fi movies where a space battleship ventures far into alien galaxies but, eventually, is reunited with the parent station, making both components whole again. Never is this umbilicus more clearly apparent than in the days leading up to the arrival of the president, His Comrade Excellency, as she calls him. She who insists on being addressed as Comrade High Commissioner.

With a state visit looming, the issue of the customary adornments had arisen yet again. She had ordered a full dress rehearsal for the president's entourage who would accompany him to the centerpiece of the ceremonies— the ceremonial dinner at Buckingham Palace, hosted by Comrade Queen Elizabeth II. The invitation issued by the flunkeys of protocol had offered national dress as a sartorial option, providing the perfect pretext for a political statement, a message to Her Majesty that her forebears' onetime imperial fief, five thousand miles to the south, at the tip of that grand continent of savannas and rain forests, the cradle of civilization, was not hers any-more.

National dress, it would be. The full fig—African style. Each individual item must be inspected for wear, tear, fit and authenticity. The blade of each assegai must be gleaming. The rounded head of each knobkerrie must be burnished. There could be no trace of moth damage from storage; no exemption, on animal welfare or any other grounds, from the obligation to wear the full outfit during the state banquet. If, as happened frequently enough, the wearer had outgrown his kit in the period since its last use, then he must diet to scale. The comrade president, himself no stripling, availed himself of a seem-ingly endless supply of leopards prepared to die in the cause of his expanding girth. But the less privileged must make the sacrifices they were called upon to make and slim down to the required dimensions in advance of the state banquet.

And that was when Stephen Nkandla launched his re-volt, having prepared the ground carefully, selected his al-lies, neutralized his rivals, wheeled and dealed.

The high commissioner had called an inspection, a roll call, in the dark, vast underground ballroom of the im-posing building on Trafalgar Square, where, in the head-ier days of virtuous protest, peace-loving activists in duffle coats had paraded with their placards and banners on the sidewalks while the representatives of the hated ra-cial state peered out on them from within and photo-graphed them for their files.

And in that spirit of the struggle for freedom, her

underlings now said: no. They would not wear traditional dress. They would wear lounge suits or even white tie and tails. But not leopard skin.

He had marshalled his arguments. Back home, he said, the codes and traditions of life were well understood. Here they were not. The climate could hardly be relied on, either, to permit such apparel. And diplomats could hardly be expected to pull on their Burberry raincoats over traditional dress in the event of a shower of rain or unforecast blizzard.

And another thing: how would this latter-day *impi* get around town? The route around The Mall and Constitution Hill was hardly the rolling veld of Zululand.

It would certainly be most inappropriate for diplomats in their full regalia to return home from the state dinner on public transport. The London subway, the tube, made no provision for cultural implements. And the sight of senior personnel in the pelts of dead animals might easily be misinterpreted, or captured on cell phone cameras and circulated, even ridiculed, on social media that would certainly come to the attention of the comrade president's office back home. There would, he said, almost inevitably, be selfies taken by scantily clad young white women sitting alongside scantily clad black diplomats. There might be scuffles with extreme rightists imagining themselves avenging Lord Chelmsford's men at Isandlwana. Or animal rights activists campaigning against the slaughter of big or any other cats. There would, quite conceivably, be arrests leading to diplomatic demarches and protests. If the British Transport Police could routinely stop and search young black men carrying hidden penknives, imagine what they would do to middle-aged black men carrying spears.

Invoking his land's hard-won democracy, for which so many had lost their lives, Stephen Nkandla called for a binding vote. Overwhelmingly, the motion was carried: traditional regalia would be optional, but the favored choice was for suit and tie, dickie bow and cummerbund. Officers of the diplomatic mission would be free to dispose—or not—of their outfits as they saw fit.

To mark his triumph, Stephen Nkandla had insisted that he be taken home, befitting his rank as deputy chief of mission, in the high commissioner's own chauffeur-driven, S-Class Mercedes with its deep leather seats and tinted glass windows and deferential local hire driver who had once worked for the special forces and now made a good living in close security.

The murderous cultural artifacts were laid reverentially in the trunk.

In the scheme of things, it was a modest triumph at best and whatever grim satisfaction he felt as the sleek, black sedan pulled out of the underground garage in Trafalgar Square evaporated not long afterward when, for all his qualifications with the SAS, driving heavily armed, stripped-down Land Rovers across the desert, and springing reflexively to the attack in the face of challenge, the chauffeur failed to spot a huge crowd of people on the street just north of the Kentish Town tube station and found the car hemmed in on all sides by people waving cell phones and shouting what sounded like religious incantations.

Stephen Nkandla could have taken the crowd in his stride. He could have sat out whatever was happening in the bulletproof, centrally locked, air-conditioned security of the big car. But, when he caught sight of an animal that he recognized as his daughter's family's pet cat, and, just behind her, a woman he recognized as his daughter's snotty neighbor, he began to sense unease.

"Let me out," he told the driver.

"It is not safe out there."

"I will be the judge of that."

The driver sighed, rolled his eyes and flicked a switch to release the dead bolts in the armored rear doors. Stephen Nkandla scanned the crowd.

"Perhaps you had better come with me," he told the chauffeur, who flipped open the trunk and slipped the knobkerrie under his jacket.

"Can't be too careful, sir," he said.

"Quite."

He had hardly advanced more than a few paces when a callow youth with notebook and pen approached him and began asking the most ridiculous questions about golf and Hitler, inquiring, too, about Stephen's name, which he had no desire to divulge to anybody.

Dolores Tremayne, in human form, clambers from the Gatwick Express and considers phoning home, but there is such a huge throng of people at Victoria Station that it hardly seems worth the effort to find space to stop and make the call so she plows gallantly on, tugging her carry-on bag behind her like a badly trained puppy. It won't be long, in any event. And maybe Gerald and the girls will be pleasantly surprised. She will be home in time for tea. She will shower to sluice off the grime of budget travel, and distribute gifts and hug everybody and cuddle the cat and know she is locked into ideal coordinates. Gently she will investigate the bizarre email from her daughter's iPad, without fuss or pulled fingernails, in that motherly way that induces confession without seeming to, third degree by stealth. Then, perhaps, when the girls are asleep, she and Gerald will reconnect and she will promise never ever ever to stay away so long again.

She considers taking a cab but figures that public transport, though less comfortable, will be much quicker.

She follows the floor-level markings that indicate the way to the tube station. Victoria line to Euston. Switch platforms for the Northern Line to Kentish Town.

Not long now.

Rosemary Saunders is frankly perplexed. The instructions were quite clear. Drop the girls at Kentish Town and see them onto the northbound C2 or 214. They have their Oyster cards, their house keys, their phones with the emergency service number preprogrammed. Police. Fire. Ambulance. They will not need any of them. They know the route, the drill, the protocols of passage through hazardous NW5 where the bad people lurk, sell drugs, have babies, eat McDonald's, pepper their protestations with expletives every second word. The bus stop they are heading for is close to home. There is a brief stretch of gentrified street, then the safe haven of the apartment. Nothing can happen to them. No trolls to leap out from under bridges, monsters to burst through the tectonic plates of planet Earth, marauding bands to sweep in on horseback from Hampstead Heath, sabers glistening, cloaks flowing. Gerald has assured her of that much at least.

So who is the man in the grubby white van, gesticulating to the girls? Why is there a stained and simply yucky mattress on the floor of the van?

Astra and Portia have been crammed into the back of Rosemary's Mercedes along with the Saunders girls. The car smells of wet dog, mud, gym kit, dubbin, a lost wedge of Brie de Meaux, Chanel No. 5. They have traveled on unfamiliar routes into the dark zones where people choose to live on top of each other, higgledy-piggledy, in apartment houses built by the local authorities, rather than in the five-or six-or more-bedroom places in luscious, leafy gardens which her husband has chosen for her and her brood.

Rosemary has gotten lost several times, forced to pull over and enter coordinates into the satnav, chart a course between rude bus drivers and motorists in old vehicles equipped with squeaky brakes and loud horns, who prefer to lower the windows rather than switch on the AC, perhaps because they smoke cigarettes and expectorate and offer ribald remarks to young female pedestrians with their hair scraped back—the Kentish Town face-lift— wearing Jeggings as if sprayed on in a paint shop. On this journey there have been old immigrant ladies pulling shopping trollies on zebra crossings where Rosemary had not planned to stop for them but who proceeded anyhow. There have been bleary, myopic eyes peering out from

Dickensian visages that show endless defeats in life's battles, marked out in pouches of pink, pale flesh and broken veins and teeth no longer capable of challenging a peach, let alone an apple; eyes that fill with resentment at the silvery car with its cargo of healthy, self-confident people whose glittery trajectory is already foretold. There has been a panicked misturn down a skanky-looking cul-de-sac that resembled a canyon of boarded-up windows and grimy lace curtains and tiny front yards filled with unspeakable sinks, toilets, washing machines, ladders, scaffolding and builders' cleft buttocks hanging from windowsills. It is perhaps this vision of nether quarters that inspires the next question.

"What does *cul* mean, Mummy?" one of the Saunders girls asks knowingly, coquettishly, with perfect French enunciation. The other Saunders girls giggle. Astra and Portia exchange swift rolled-eyed glances.

"Not now, dear. Google it," Rosemary replies, reversing hectically between parked cars, narrowly avoiding the creation of an evidential trail of wing-mirrors and insurance claims. And yet more scrapes, dings, dents, scratches to annoy her husband.

"Google, not giggle," Rosemary says—an adage for life delivered with a dollop of tart rebuke. No one speaks for a bit. There is a honking of car horns as the big Mercedes station wagon hurtles backward out of the cul-de-sac into the flow of traffic, past the signs warning motorists that they are entering a dead-end, bereft of egress.

"Bottom," another of the Saunders girls says suddenly.

"Bum," says another.

"Arse."

"For Christ's sake. What do they teach you at that school?"

"French, Mama. *Le Français.*"

But now they are at the handover point designated by the handsome first novelist and househusband (who, as we know—but Rosemary cannot—is quite close by).

Since the people from Neighborhood Watch came by to explain the criminal classes to the chattering classes, Rosemary has sought to hone her powers of observation and she has come up with weasely, or at least rodentesque, to describe the man with the white van who is speaking to her, his words borne on waves of breath that make you wonder where exactly he has been feeding. There is a tattoo on his hand that resembles a swastika. He is wearing an army-surplus combat jacket. Hardly the type of person, Rosemary thinks, to be consorting with. But then, these days, one could never tell. Or, at least, never admit to knowing the distinction between the real people and the rest.

"My daughter, see?" he is saying. "Sharon. A devil for the computer. Always on it. Me I can take it or leave. Internet. But she's a devil for it."

"So where is she now? Sharon?" Rosemary knows she sounds snooty and is making a conscious effort to sound infinitely more superior, if only to mask the lurching queasiness that she is experiencing. She has clambered out of the car.

Portia and Astra have followed her.

"Ah there you are, Porsche," the man says, "Recognize you from the photo you sent my Sharon. Hop in."

He takes her by the arm as if to propel her toward the white van.

This is a new twist, Gerald is thinking. Maybe I am in over my head. Maybe I have overreached myself.

With the panache of a vaudeville magician Mathilde de Villeneuve has produced from her cleavage a silvery, ornate, spoon-like item that now brims with white powder. Presto! With her seat belt unlocked, she leans over the central console of the mighty beast and positions it under his nose.

"Snort," she instructs.

He has already reached the point of sneezing from his previous ingestions but contrives to contain his hungry nostrils and follow her instructions. Thank the Lord for tinted glass windows, he is thinking. Vaguely, as they pass by the old Blustons store where ladies of a certain age bought frocks of a certain vintage, and the Mediterranean food shop and the pub that is always being revamped and, finally, the approaches to the tube station, he is aware of the traffic lights changing, separated from him by an unusual expanse of empty road (save for a couple of Lycra-clad cyclists—but they do not really count). The powder closes down some cognitive pathways, but opens up others designed for pleasure. The color signals jumble. Can red really mean halt, danger?

A deep sniff with one hand on the steering wheel while the other uses the facility of the opposable thumb to pinch one nostril closed so that he is able to inhale abruptly, satisfyingly through the other.

Sniff sniff vroom vroom.

The beast leaps forward.

His nose has begun to run a little.

Not too far behind him, another color. Blue. Flashing blue. Better put some distance between the Range Rover and the source of the siren sound. This is definitely not the time to get busted. Not with this wild cargo on board.

"Seat belt," he commands. For some reason he thinks of that scene in the film about a great white shark where one of the actors says: "They're all going to die."

"Fasten seat belts," he repeats. "This could get hairy."

She obeys. Grins.

Yay!

Jaws.

That one did not end happily, either. For the fish or the skipper out to catch it.

On the moving staircase with her carry-on tucked neatly against her legs, Dolores is aware of some excitement among her fellow travelers. Far more people than usual have left the train at Kentish Town. They are clutching smartphones and she catches incomprehensible references to signal strengths and hashtags. There is a bustle in the air, a sense of expectation, anticipation. Probably some weird concert at the Forum, that vast cavern where she and Gerald watched Ian Dury's last gig and where people in all manner of bizarre clothing and hairstyle and skin piercings gather for arcane communion with cult-like bands. Sex and drugs and rock and roll. But no one is talking music or performers. She could swear she keeps on hearing the word "cat."

Reg Crouch cannot make head nor tail of it, either.

Well, the tail is evident, as is the head, in fact, but an understanding of the causal link between this bushy cat's extremities and the crowd behind it eludes him completely. Breathlessly he dictates frantic notes into the record facility of his smartphone. Vast crowd. All races. Police escort. Happy-clappers. Hallelujah. Hippies. Webby peeps. Approaching Kentish Town tube. Destination unclear.

The intrepid reporter jogs along the fringes of the crowd. Must be hundreds of them. Better make that thousands. To be on the safe side.

He calls in.

"Really weird," he tells his news editor, who barks back: "I can fucking see that. Get me quotes. Color. File soonest. File oftenest." Clearly, Reg thinks, his boss has regressed to some pre-internet age when cablese dictated curious usages to save on transmission costs charged by the word.

The Golden Age. Trench coats. Trilby hats. Bush jackets and vast expense accounts in the tropics, in the battle zones. Typewriters and cleft sticks.

Why you unswim sharkinfestedwaters? Frontwise soonest!

How seeing crowd?

Reg glances skyward, his attention seized by the clatter of a helicopter emblazoned with the logo of a twenty-four-hour news channel that is doubtless providing breathless live coverage to TV sets across the nation, including the ginormous fifty-inch HD jobby in the newsroom to which his editor is forever glued. Must be big, he thinks, to merit the chopper. Could be big for me, too. The big break. Finally. "*Sun* Reporter Uncovers Cat Cult." "Feline Frolics Frenzy." Scoop!

"What's its name?" he asks a woman who is jogging alongside him at the head of the ever-expanding crowd.

"Fucking cat!" Jenny Steinem shrieks in reply. "Fucking, fucking, awful fucking cat."

"Funny name," Reg shouts back, his voice battling against the decibel wave of rotor blades, police sirens, hallelujahs.

"X," the woman shouts, her reddening face close to his. "X. X. X. Fucking X."

"Sex?"

Most of her gabbled reply is lost but he catches "pregnant" and his mind boggles.

"Feline Fertility Frenzy in Cat Cult Sexcapade. Sex Cat Shocker!"

"No Nazis? Golf?" he says in what he imagines to be a suave and worldly-sounding follow-up, recalling his boss's offer of a bonus in return for those prized elements.

"Nazi Sex Cat in Golf Fertility Scam."

"What?" the woman screams. "Are you insane?"

But Reg has jogged forward for a better view. Ever the intrepid newshound. "Cat Made Me Pregnant, Says Nazi Golf Champ." He had forgotten to ask her name, he realized. But that was a minor point. A trivial factoid like a real name could really hamper the processes of news creation. "Cottaging Cat Tells All." "Tabby Tees Off Hitler Revival Tourney." "Moggy Made Me Mum, Says Nazi Golf Jogger." "Pussy Galore in Sex Kitten Cover-up." The possibilities were endless.

At the roadside, he sees a large black Mercedes, hemmed in by the crowd, unable to move. The rear door opens. A patrician-looking man in an elegant dark suit clambers out, accompanied by a mean, muscled character concealing a cudgel, scanning the chaotic scenes that are being witnessed. Reg approaches and asks his name, but before he can run through the interviewer's litany of questions—who, why, how, where, when, what, and how much shall I write this check for?—his cell phone rings and the display shows him that it is his superior calling for an update.

"Any Nazis yet?" the editor shouts.

"Not really," Reg replies.

Stephen Nkandla has espied a silver estate car and a rusty white van and begins to trot toward them, moving with surprising speed and nimbleness, outpacing even the cat. The chauffeur lopes alongside. In his mind, he is crossing the barren lands on the approaches to Baghdad. The training has kicked in. The responses to whatever will happen have been programmed in on training missions in the Brecon Beacons and remote regions of Kenya. Whatever happens now has been foretold in the manuals that teach young soldiers how to kill with a rolled-up newspaper.

"There's a weird-looking guy here," Reg is telling his editor. "He's carrying a club."

"Did you say *golf club*?" the editor asks him in something approaching awe. "Well I'll be . . ." but his words are lost in the clatter of the helicopter's rotor blades and the roar of the crowd.

The man Rosemary Saunders has identified as comparable to a ferret, stoat or weasel, or possibly a rat, seems to be slowly concluding that things are not going exactly according to plan.

"Do you actually have a daughter called Sharon?" Rosemary asks imperiously.

"She said she'd be here herself," Portia says, digging in her heels, embracing Astra with the one arm to which the verminous figure is not clinging. She feels his grasp loosen. She sees a look of alarm cross his face. The sound of police sirens is getting closer. But that is not all.

Around a corner to the north, he is aware of a sudden bedlam, a pullulating throng of people to all intents and purposes following a cat. A cat that now seems to have zeroed in on him. A cat that is sprinting at an impossible pace, pursued by the baying crowd. Is this what foxhunting looks like? Massive numbers in pursuit of a single quarry? But that is not what is happening here. The cat is leading. The pied pussy of Hamelin. It is leading the horde toward the single rat. It is sprinting. It has crossed the road. It stops. It surveys the scene before it. The congregation behind it stops too. People collide with the people in front, like a highway pileup, but no one remonstrates or threatens lawsuits. For a second the frame freezes. No one moves or speaks. The silence is incomplete because of the clattering helicopter up above. Reg Crouch is reminded of those frustrating moments when you are trying to stream videos and movement gives way to buffering. Then the cat lowers itself to the ground. Its haunches sway. Its feather-duster tail flicks from side to side. The muscles bunch in its rear legs. Don't stop now, Dolores is screaming silently. For God's sake, X, do something.

X does just that.

Like a Top Gun missile locked on to its target, X hurtles forward, propelled by unimaginable forces. Closing on her target, she leaps into flight. Her needle fangs sink into his arm. Red in tooth and claw. Forget the fox. The hunter is now the hunted. The tables are turned on the preying predator. Through her cat's eyes, Dolores has a front-row seat. She is on the flight deck of justice. And she understands.

X has saved the day—and the daughter—in a way that the inner Dolores, bereft of motor facilities, could not. X is not just some cat. She is the avenging sword. X as in Excalibur, so bright in the enemy's eyes that it blinded him.

Ferret, stoat, or weasel is afraid. It has all gone pear-shaped. Weeks, months of grooming gone to waste. At the very moment of the snatch. The pain in his arm is indescribable. The cat has jaws of iron and incisors sharper than a dentist's drill, puncturing skin, sliding into veins and arteries, grinding toward bone.

He releases Portia.

The cat releases him.

He leaps into his white van and turns the key to cajole the tired, rumbly, reluctant diesel into action. It takes a while. Siren noise grows louder. Crowd approaching.

Strangers. Faces. Black man accompanied by murderous white man. With club. Voices. What's all this then?

Some callow youth with a smartphone starts asking him questions about golf and Hitler.

The engine catches and he slams the gear lever and slips the clutch all in one blind moment. At least the lights are not red, he thinks as the van lurches forward and to his right he is suddenly aware of onrushing chrome and steel and blue paintwork and a huge impact that knocks his old white van onto its rusting flank with deafening noises of grating, rending metal. The van scrapes and screeches along the road, gored by the roaring Range Rover, and he is lying on his side with his blood seeping through the shattered window onto the highway and he knows he is going to die or at least go to jail and thinks that, of the two, death would probably be preferable.

"It's Daddy! He came to save us," Portia exclaims, seeing the Range Rover.

"But who's that with him?" Astra inquires.

"And what are those big white bags in the car?"

"And why is that man with Granddad bashing Daddy's car?"

Dolores with her roll-on, business class–sized cabin baggage feels as if she has been ejected out of the entrance to the Kentish Town tube station like a stopper from a bottle, surrounded by many other stoppers, all popping simultaneously. Somehow, as the escalator rose up from deep-belowground tracks, a mass, collective urge seemed to grasp her and her fellow travelers, drawn to noise and mayhem outside, pulling them, molding them into a unit that overcame the exit barriers and surged forward only to come to an abrupt halt at a scene of incomprehensible chaos.

At first, her cognitive faculties are overwhelmed by a barrage of random impressions. For instance, she sees her daughters and X, the cat. And Rosemary Saunders, the school busybody/super soccer mom. She sees the family car, its front end mangled and shoving up against the oily, messy underside of another vehicle, which has capsized, spilling fluids onto the road. She sees her husband pinioned by a big white air bag. He seems to be nodding and shrugging and trying to smile. But next to him is a stranger, also trapped by an air bag. A stranger dressed as a pole dancer. And outside the car, a man accompanying her own father is using a cultural implement to launch alternating onslaughts against the battered van and the stricken Range Rover.

Some kind of rescue?

But none of these perceptions have any substance that might explain the scene around them.

For instance, there is a great crowd of people. Some of them are busy tweeting and WhatsApping and Snapchatting on their phones. Others have burst into a hymn to praise the Lord. There is a helicopter thwacking the air overhead. And police officers looking bemused, calling for backup—fire service, ambulance, paramedics, social services, and, more surreptitiously, contacts in the news media known to pay handsomely for tip-offs. There is her neighbor, Jenny Steinem, standing next to the wreck of the family Range Rover, shouting at the trapped woman, as if berating her.

In front of her, a young man on a mobile phone is saying: "That's it, chief. Right. 'Family Cat Thwarts Sex Fiend.' What? No. No Nazis or anything. We got a bloke with a swastika tattoo. Not enough? Fair enough. Sorry. Yeah. What? Okay. If you like. You can call it a golf club if you like. I mean, at this stage, who's going to argue?"

Dolores Tremayne crosses the road and embraces her daughters. X, the family cat, leaps into her arms and peers into her eyes. She is transfixed by this gaze. She sees other eyes, frantic, like a prisoner's, behind the cat's blue retinae, which have locked on to her, unblinking, and she cannot help but feel that she is caught up in some kind of upload-download data-switch in which terabytes of the most unwholesome material are being transferred from her cat into the depths of her soul. She reels, staggers slightly, as this avalanche of unprocessed images which she never wished to see—many of them extremely lewd—fills her mind like a living nightmare. There are snatches of conversation, dramas she cannot understand involving flight and hiding and the cat flap and dogs and the face of a pretty young woman framed in the portcullis of the cat-box.

She is the feline confessor—forgive me, Mother, for I have witnessed sin against you. She is X's debrief officer. And then what happened? You have done well, Agent X. What else did you see?

On the fringes of the crowd, Rosemary Saunders is already on the phone to the soccer mom's support society, giving chapter and verse. "I'm not saying it's anything to do with skin color," she is saying. "But, well . . . no smoke without fire. Yes, I did say a club. Her father, I think. And the other one? Some kind of stripper, by the look of it. It's those poor girls I feel sorry for." Her interlocutors are spellbound. So just imagine, they will say forever more, Dolores Tremayne's husband was caught with an erotic dancer with a golf club of all things! At least that's what it will say in the papers.

Her daughters study the sudden unscheduled apparition of this person they know as their mother and see that she is staring intently at X, sometimes nodding as if absorbing a fine point in a legal argument, sometimes raising her eyebrows in shock or surprise. Sometimes she breaks her communion with the cat to glance at her husband and the neighbor and the jazzy woman next to him in the car whose face seems dusted in white powder, rather like one of those old-fashioned circus clowns. When she is transfixed by the cat, her expression is intense, interrogatory, understanding, beyond shock, essentially warm, betraying a kind of intimacy without words or purrs. But when she surveys her husband and his companion and their neighbor—knowing now what she has learned—her eyes turn blank and cold. And when her eyes roam over her lovely daughters, she wants at once to go home with them to cuddle but not to go home to the arena of betrayal.

"Excuse me, madam." It is a police officer.

"Do you know the gentleman in the Range Rover?"

"I did once," she says. "Or at least I thought I did."

"And the lady?"

"Only generically."

"And the gentleman with the club?"

"Not really. But by the way . . ."

"Yes, madam?"

"The club?"

"Yes, madam?"

"It's a cultural implement."

"Of course, madam."

Inside the overturned white van, the man with the swastika—his name, as it is given on the sex offenders' list, is Lionel Jones, but he has other aliases—knows that he has finally run out of escape routes. He has no daughter called Sharon. His wife and two sons left him long ago after the first conviction. He lives alone in a rented studio apartment across the way from a primary school. The name on the short lease is John Gillingham. His laptop, his HD movie camera, and his binoculars are pretty much his only possessions of any value. And once the police get into the laptop with its massive harvest from the dark web, the case will be open and shut. Send him down, the judge will say, without the option of parole or remission. Forgive me, Father, he thinks—a snippet of God talk linked irrevocably to the memory of the first exploratory touchings of his cassocked confessor. Lying in his van with a variety of superficial wounds oozing small amounts of blood, he is vaguely hoping that he has suffered some terminal internal injury that he cannot yet feel because of the adrenaline rush. Anything, he figures, will be better than being sent back inside where the other prisoners have their own ways of dealing with his kind. There is a terrible racket in his ears as the emergency services go to work with a huge whirring circular saw to extricate him from the wreckage—the opening bars of the music he will have to face. Someone else seems to be beating on his van with some kind of club, as if it were an infernal kettledrum. He wishes they would all go away. He wishes to be left alone. Forever. But that cannot be.

The Range Rover is hosting a different drama, three acts in one. Mathilde de Villeneuve has recovered her composure. She has located her cell phone and has called in the cavalry—a firm of lawyers specializing in the art of the super-injunction. Already the advocates have set many clocks ticking and dispatched a representative—posthaste—to the scene of the alleged incident in which their client has been an unwitting and wholly innocent bystander. M'lud. Senior partners are launching the tele-phonic equivalent of a Grad missile onslaught to various mainstream media editors and website operators to en-sure that no mention is made of her. Surprisingly, at one tabloid where the upholders of the law and beneficiaries of the legal system usually expect resistance and counter-attacks, their interlocutor seeks guarantees from them that the super-injunction does not cover reporting of golf, Nazis or cats. Once satisfied on that score, the news editor—a bastion of journalistic probity—agrees to the terms of the order about to be issued by a compliant judge. Not only will there be no mention of Mathilde de Villeneuve, there will be no mention of the order pre-venting publication of her name, image or any form of identification. Webbie types go to work with their pix-elation tools. Photoshop will do for the rest. Publicly, Mathilde has ceased to exist.

But not Gerald Tremayne. As a precaution, he has quickly swallowed the rest of his stash, figuring erroneously that, with any luck, a mild cardiac episode will win him a sympathy vote and head off close scrutiny by the increasing numbers of perplexed law enforcement officers milling around. To his amazement, Mathilde de Ville-neuve has wriggled free of the air bag and transferred herself to the rear seat of the vehicle, opened her carry-on bag and with remarkable speed changed her clothing into a houndstooth business suit. Through the still intact rearview mirror, he watches, transfixed by her quick thinking and decisive actions, as she rearranges her hair, removes the more excessive flourishes of her artiste's makeup and puts on a pair of dark glasses. Shielded from public view by the tinted rear windows, and carrying only a handbag stuffed with essential accoutrements— passports, credit cards, bearer bonds, jewelry, and cash in large denominations of several currencies—she scram-bles over the backseat into the voluminous luggage com-partment, where she activates the emergency locking device to slide out of the Range Rover and disappear among crowds of people too distracted by the overall drama to absorb the full significance of such minutiae.

To look at her, Gerald thinks, you'd think she was born and raised to the ways of evading detection and arrest. And probably, she was. She has gone. Jumped ship. Scar-pered. Flown the coop. Just as he would, if he could.

He is alone in the car, but not in the world.

Outside the driver's side window, Stephen Nkandla's face is set in a rictus of rage. Gerald cannot hear what his father-in-law is saying but he understands well enough the general drift. I knew, from the beginning, that you were a scoundrel, a mountebank, a charlatan, a rogue, a villain. White trash! I knew you were not worthy of my daughter. And now you have brought eternal shame upon us.

Through the crowds, Gerald notices a lithe, muscled man wearing a chauffeur's uniform and carrying an African-looking club. He has been beating on the side of the white van as if he wished to destroy its relative symmetry forever. But now he is elbowing his way forward, nodding in a familiar sort of way to the senior police officers on the scene. There is some discussion between them. A decision is being weighed, though Gerald cannot know this, between the illegality of abetting the departure of a witness from the scene of a crime and a diplomatic incident that will bring all kind of besuited intercessions at Scotland Yard from the mandarins of the Foreign and Commonwealth Office in King Charles Street. Wisdom prevails. The chauffeur approaches the father-in-law. Better leave now while we can, sir, he is saying. Don't want to cause all kinds of démarches and whatnot, do we, sir? He conceals the short, stubby knob-kerrie under his jacket. He leads the crestfallen warrior away. There will be another day. Another Isandlwana. You haven't heard the last of this, Stephen Nkandla calls back over his shoulder. Already his chauffeur-savior is on his phone, phoning the embassy's legal attaché to ensure that a word is had with people who know how to put the genie back in the bottle. It will be a good day for the lawyers.

Though not, as noted earlier, for Gerald Tremayne.

He does not know how his wife knows all that she knows. But he knows she knows everything. It is something to do with the cat, evidently, the cat that led the bipeds in a merry dance all the way to Kentish Town tube station. The cat that spied on him, tailed him, infiltrated his secret domain. Nibbled his prophylactic. Enraged his all-too-irascible mistress, who has now turned on her heels and is walking back toward the apartment house, stiff with humiliation and vengeful fury.

The cat that spilled the beans to his wife.

How had she known to return precisely at this moment of cathartic craziness? Should she not be high above the Atlantic, en route to Detroit?

Through the windscreen he looks balefully at Dolores and his two daughters and their cat, all interwoven with arms and paws. His novelist's inventive imagination offers him best-case scenarios. He will explain all. His side of the story. Cats can be mistaken, you know, honey. They don't see things like you and me. Nothing really happened. I did not have sex with that woman. Well, okay, just a bit. Almost a virgin. And the entertainer? An old friend from before. Just giving her a lift.

From Heathrow? On a school day?

But I saved the day. Knight in shining armor. Broadsided the bounder. Rescued our daughter from a fate worse than death.

You mean Rosemary Saunders? Your partner in this venture? Another of your trophies? And how, for God's sake, had it gotten this far with some pedophile pervert about to make off with her in broad daylight?

Contrition. Full disclosure. The only route. Counseling. Addictive personality, Your Honor. He looked again at Dolores and knew from her granite glare that it would not wash. Over Dolores's shoulder, beyond the crowds and the policemen and the fire trucks and the news crews, his Wordsworthian inner eye that will be the bliss of future solitude conjured the bleak reaches of the M1 highway unfurling northward through endless snarl-ups and speed traps and trucks, past Milton Keynes and Watford Gap and Northampton and Leeds—all the way back to where he had started in the northeast, a small-town dealer who had stumbled into the limelight, dazzled and doomed.

Maybe his face in the news would help sales. Genius in freefall. Icarus.

Maybe there was a book in it.

And then again.

Maybe not.

As if waking from a dream, Stephen Nkandla breaks away from his chauffeur's solicitous, guiding hand and hurries to his daughter's side. He embraces two generations of his descendants. Plus a cat. He gestures to his driver to prepare the Mercedes for the getaway, shepherding his tribe away. A tyro paparazzo raises a camera but there is a lightning flash of a knobkerrie and it falls to the ground in several pieces. A man in a chauffeur's traditional dress—dark suit, white shirt, black tie—retrieves the data card from the debris. Then the family members are piling into the plush cocoon of the car—Dolores and her girls in the rear seat, her father riding shotgun up front. X is experiencing strange things. A burden has been lifted; a demon has been excised from deep within, though she has lost the ability to articulate such notions.

The last Gerald sees of his family is the cameo of his daughters' puzzled and tearful faces, framed in the rear window of the big black car as it pulls into the thinning crowd and nudges forward. And the last vision they have of him on that awful day of rescue and recrimination is of a police officer prizing open the door of his crumpled chariot and leading him away.

epilogue

They took a long break, the three of them, leaving X with her parents, and Gerald to his own devices.

Everyone, suddenly, seemed to have a lot more time on their hands.

To the satisfaction of her father—now enjoying early retirement far more than he had anticipated—she chose southern Africa as her destination. Victoria Falls. Chobe game reserve. Paddling in makoro wooden canoes through the Okavango Delta, amid crocs. Locations chosen not so much as routes to her roots, but as places that were a long, long way from North London, Munich, Detroit, Osaka, Kentish Town, Gerald.

Her employers had seized gleefully on her public misfortune to suggest that she depart the company forthwith and cash in her stock options in lieu of payment, thank you very much. But after very confidential verbal exchanges with her—revolving around her knowledge of the whereabouts and content of encrypted emissions software concealed in safety deposit boxes—they had agreed to write a glowing reference for the benefit of prospective bosses, reinforced by generous amounts of severance pay.

She refused to sign a nondisclosure agreement.

Trust me, she told them with a smile. She had the drop on them. For once.

Dolores and Portia and Astra traveled on southward. They flew some of the way. They drove other bits, on long ribbons of highway that unfurled through brittle savanna where people in ragged clothes offered small pyramids of tomatoes and corn for sale at the roadside. They took an overnight luxury train. Portia said she was sorry and wept bitterly. And Dolores told her she had nothing to apologize for. She had been lonely. Her kindness had been taken advantage of. By a very bad man. She would not be lonely again.

Astra asked if she could have a puppy and Dolores said she would seek X's permission.

At the back of the mother's mind, there was the question of permanent removal to these southerly latitudes, once charted by navigators on their way to the East Indies. She contemplated real estate agents' brochures and translated the local money into her own kind of money and figured she could afford a whole mansion, not just a mansion flat. Portia and Astra accompanied her with no apparent enthusiasm—indeed, with deep suspicion—to several sunlit schools where everyone seemed to play sport like Olympians against the backdrop of a famous, craggy, flat-topped mountain.

"Can we go home now?" Portia asked.

"Not this new home? Here? In Africa?" Dolores said.

"Real home," Astra said. "Where Daddy is."

"We'll see," Dolores replied, although she has already decided on her course of action.

Indeed, her lawyers are drawing up the paperwork in her absence and when he receives them, Gerald will probably count himself lucky that the visitation terms are so generous, even if his alimony is so modest as to enforce lifestyle changes on a significant scale. No more Range Rover. No more dizzy highs. Quite a lot of lows. And bus journeys. And abstinence.

Still, the outcome has not been all bad. After the debacle at Kentish Town, the cops agreed to look the other way on the matter of certain quantities of alleged class-A drugs—personal use only, m'lud—and focus on sending down John Gillingham, aka Lionel Jones, for as long as possible. Gerald's clients for his trade in the aforementioned narcotics bolted to safer suppliers. His mistresses, too. Jenny Steinem did not even call when she moved out of her apartment—after a quiet but unmistakably ominous word from Dolores—and flew back to America. There has been the question of a motoring misdemeanor—driving without due care and attention, failing to halt at a traffic signal—but that did not merit a mention in the press. Intrepidly, Reg Crouch tried to interest his news editor, but the hoary veteran just told him with a wheeze that could have been laughter: "No point flogging a dead Nazi, Reg. Not even with a golf club."

Once, in a newsagent's shop, Gerald espied a copy of *Hello!* magazine proclaiming the marriage-made-in-heaven of a billionaire named Mark Danvers and an heiress called Mathilde de Villeneuve. The cover photograph of her in a luminous white wedding dress with train and veil coaxed a rare, wan smile. The virgin Madonna. And mark. Her new husband. Mark by name, mark by destiny.

He understood, now, how *Marriage*—in fact, marriage—ended. He did not relish writing it. But, in his rented "garden" flat, whose security-barred windows offered a sunless prospect of the lower legs of people scurrying by in the rain and early, wintry darkness on the sidewalk above him, he knew he would try hard, stabbing at his laptop, before *Death* was all that was left on his agenda.

This time, he printed out his chapters as he finished them and was pleased with the slowly mounting pile of typescript.

All work and no play. That was his life now.

And X? What happened to X?

She was found in a pool of blood where Astra's puppy, which had turned out to be a pit bull, not a poodle as the pet store owner insisted, snapped her neck in a fit of bloodlust and feasted on the furry repast.

No. That is not what really happened. Thank goodness! That is Gerald's dream of what should happen when X figure-of-eights through his legs and looks up at him with a kind of vague, mocking recognition on those prescribed days when he may visit with his daughters or fix a leaky tap in their kitchen or escort them to their new school in a different part of town where their story—like all our stories—is theirs to invent.

about the author

ALAN S. COWELL is a British writer whose career spanned four decades as a foreign correspondent, first for Reuters and then for *The New York Times*. Alongside news coverage, he authored works of fiction and nonfiction, including *The Terminal Spy*, a definitive account of the life and death of Alexander V. Litvinenko, a former KGB officer poisoned with radioactive polonium in London in 2006.